At a cafe in Budapest, Oswald, a British ambassador in his thirties, meets the young, handsome Imre, a Hungarian military officer. The two develop a strong friendship through their shared interest in art, but as their relationship grows more serious, they begin spending hours upon hours sharing their innermost secrets.

Eventually, their friendship turns to romance, a partnership between equals who respect and cherish one another despite the obstacles of an intensely homophobic society.

Published in a time when homosexuality was largely criminalized, Imre: A Memorandum offered a hopeful narrative immersed in gay history that would prove both inspiring and instructional for generations to come.

First published 1906 in a private edition by the author.

This edition first published by Fahrenheit Press 2023

ISBN: 978-1-914475-54-2

10 9 8 7 6 5 4 3 2 1

www.Fahrenheit-Press.com

F 4 E

Cover Design & Manuscript Typesetting by www.SkullStarStudio.com

Imre: A Memorandum

By

Edward Prime-Stevenson

Fahrenheit Press

You have spoken of homosexualism, that profound problem in human nature of old or of to-day; noble or ignoble; outspoken or masked; never to be repressed by religions nor philosophies nor laws; which more and more is demanding the thought of all modern civilizations, however unwillingly accorded it..... Its diverse aspects bewilder me... Homosexualism is a symphony running through a marvellous range of psychic keys, with many high and heroic (one may say divine) harmonies; but constantly relapsing to base and fantastic discords!... Is there really now, as ages ago, a sexual aristocracy of the male? A mystic and hellenic Brotherhood, a sort of super-virile man? A race with hearts never to be kindled by any woman; though, if once aglow, their strange fires can burn not less ardently and purely than ours? An élite in passion, conscious of a superior knowledge of Love, initiated into finer joys and pains than ours?—that looks down with pity and contempt on the millions of men wandering in the valleys of the sexual commonplace?

– Magyarból

PREFATORY

My dear Mayne:

In these pages I give you a chapter out of my life... an episode that at first seemed impossible to write even to you. It has lengthened under my hand, as autobiography is likely to do. My apology is that in setting forth absolute truth in which we ourselves are concerned so deeply, the perspectives, and what painters call the values, are not easily maintained. But I hope not to be tedious to the reader for whom, especially, I have laid open as mysterious and profoundly personal an incident.

You know why it has been written at all for you. Now that it lies before me, finished, I do not feel so dubious of what may be thought of its utterly sincere course as I did when I began to put it on paper. And as you have more than once urged me to write something concerning just that topic which is the mainspring of my pages I have asked myself whether, instead of some impersonal essay, I would not do best to give over to your editorial hand all that is here?—as something for other men than for you and me only? Do with it, therefore, as you please. As speaking out to any other human heart that is throbbing on in rebellion against the ignorances, the narrow psychologic conventions, the false social ethics of our epoch—too many men's hearts must do so!—as offered in a hope that some perplexed and solitary soul may grow a little calmer, may feel itself a little less alone in our world of mysteries—so do I give this record to you, to use it as you will. Take it as from Imre and from me.

As regards the actual narrative, I may say to you here that the dialogue is kept, word for word, faithfully as it passed, in all the more significant passages; and that the correspondence is literally translated.

I do not know what may be the exact shade of even your sympathetic judgment, as you lay down the manuscript, read. But, for myself, I put by my pen after the last lines were written, with two lines of Platen in my mind that had often recurred to me during the progress of my record: as a hope, a trust, a conviction:

> *Ist's möglich ein Geschöpf in der Natur zu sein,*
> *Und stets und wiederum auf falscher Spur zu sein?*

Or, as the question of the poet can be put into English:

> *Can one created be—of Nature part—*
> *And ever, ever trace a track that's false?*

No... I do not believe it!

Faithfully yours,
Oswald.

I. MASKS.

Like flash toward metal, magnet sped to iron,
A Something goes—a Current, mystic, strange—
From man to man, from human breast to breast:
Yet 'tis not Beauty, Virtue, Grace, not Truth
That binds nor shall unbind, that magic tie.
— GRILLPARZER

It was about four o' clock that summer afternoon, that I sauntered across a street in the cheerful Hungarian city of Szent-Istvánhely, and turned aimlessly into the café-garden of the Erzsébet-tér, where the usual vehement military-band concert was in progress. I looked about for a free table, at which to drink an iced-coffee, and to mind my own business for an hour or so. Not in a really cross-grained mood was I; but certainly dull, and preoccupied with perplexing affairs left loose in Vienna; and little inclined to observe persons and things for the mere pleasure of doing so.

The kiosque-garden was somewhat crowded. At a table, a few steps away, sat only one person; a young Hungarian officer in the pale blue-and-fawn of a lieutenant of the well-known A— Infantry Regiment. He was not reading, though at his hand lay one or two journals. Nor did he appear to be bestowing any great amount of attention on the chattering around him, in that distinctively Szent-Istvánhely manner which ignores any kind of outdoor musical entertainment as a thing to be listened-to. An open letter was lying beside him, on a chair; but he was not heeding that. I turned his way; we exchanged the usual sacramental saluts, in which attention I met the glance, by no means welcoming, of a pair of peculiarly brilliant but not shadowless hazel eyes; and I sat down for my coffee. I remember that I had a swift, general impression that my neighbour was of no ordinary beauty of physique and elegance of bearing, even in a land where such matters are normal details of personality. And somehow it was also borne in upon me promptly that his mood

3

was rather like mine. But this was a vague concern. What was Hecuba to me?—or Priam, or Helen, or Helenus, or anybody else, when for the moment I was so out of tune with life!

Presently, however, the band began playing (with amazing calmness from any Hungarian wind-orchestra) Roth's graceful "Frau Réclame" Waltz, then a novelty, of which trifle I happen to be fond. Becoming interested in the leader, I wanted to know his name. I looked across the table at my vis-à-vis. He was pocketing the letter. With a word of apology, which turned his face to me, I put the inquiry. I met again the look, this time full, and no longer unfriendly, of as winning and sincere a countenance, a face that was withal strikingly a temperamental face, as ever is bent toward friend or stranger. And it was a Magyar voice, that characteristically seductive thing in the seductive race, which answered my query; a voice slow and low, yet so distinct, and with just that vibrant thrill lurking in it which instantly says something to a listener's heart, merely as a sound, if he be susceptible to speaking-voices. A few commonplaces followed between us, as to the band, the programme, the weather—each interlocutor, for no reason that he could afterward explain, any more than can one explain thousands of such attitudes of mind during casual first meetings—taking a sort of involuntary account of the other. The commonplaces became more real exchanges of individual ideas. Evidently, this Magyar fellow-idler, in the Erzsébet-tér café, was in a social frame of mind, after all. As for myself, indifference to the world in general and to my surroundings in particular, dissipated and were forgot, my disgruntled and egotistical humour went to the limbo of all unwholesomenesses, under the charm of that musical accent, and in the frank sunlight of those manly, limpid eyes. There was soon a regular dialogue in course, between this stranger and me. From music (that open road to all sorts of mutualities on short acquaintanceships) and an art of which my neighbour showed that he knew much and felt even more than he expressed—from music, we passed to one or another aesthetic question; to literature, to social life, to human relationships, to human emotions. And thus, more and more, by unobserved advances, we came onward to our own two lives and beings. The only interruptions, as that long and clear afternoon lengthened about us, occurred when some military or civil acquaintance of my incognito passed him, and gave a greeting. I spoke of my birth-land, to which I was nowadays so much a stranger. I sketched some of the long and rather goal-less wanderings, almost always alone, that I had made in Central Europe and the Nearer East—his country growing, little by little, my special haunt. I found myself charting-out to him what things I liked and what things I anything but liked, in this world where most of us must be satisfied to wish for considerably more than we receive. And in return, without any more questions from me than I had from him—each of us carried along by that irresistible undercurrent of human intercourse that is indeed, the Italian simpatia, by the quick confidence that one's instinct assures him is neither lightly-bestowed, after all, nor lightly-taken—did I begin, during even those first hours of our coming-together, to know no small part of the inner individuality of Imre von N..., hadnagy (Lieutenant) in the A... Honvéd Regiment, stationed during some years in Szent-Istvánhely.

Lieutenant Imre's concrete story was an exceedingly simple matter. It was the everyday outline of the life of nine young Magyar officers in ten. He was twenty-five; the only son of an old Transylvanian family; one poor now as never before, but evidently quite as proud as ever. He had had other notions, as a lad, of a calling. But the men of the N.... line had always been in the army, ever since the days of Szigetvár and the Field of Mohács. Soldiers, soldiers! always soldiers! So he had graduated at the Military Academy. Since then? Oh, mostly routine-life, routine work... a few professional journeyings in the provinces—no advancement and poor pay, in a country where an officer must live particularly like a gentleman; if too frequently only with the aid of confidential business-interviews with Jewish usurers. He sketched his happenings in the barracks or the ménage—and his own simple, social interests, when in Szent-Istvánhely. He did not live with his people, who were in too remote a quarter of the town for his duties. I could see that even if he were rather removed from daily contact with the family-affairs, the present home atmosphere was a depressing one, weighing much on his spirits. And no wonder! In the beginning of a brilliant career, the father had become blind and was now a pensioned officer, with a shattered, irritable mind as well as body, a burden to everyone about him. The mother had been a beauty and rich. Both her beauty and riches long ago had departed, and her health with them. Two sisters were dead, and two others had married officials in modest Government stations in distant cities. There were more decided shadows than lights in the picture. And there came to me, now and then, as it was sketched, certain inferences that made it a thought less promising. I guessed the speaker's own nervous distaste for a profession arbitrarily bestowed on him. I caught his something too-passionate half-sigh for the more ideal daily existence, seen always through the dust of the dull highroad that often does not seem likely ever to lead one out into the open. I noticed traces of weakness in just the ordinary armour a man needs in making the most of his environment, or in holding-out against its tyrannies. I saw the irresolution, the doubts of the value of life's struggle, the sense of fatality as not only a hindrance but as excuse. Not in mere curiosity so much as in sympathy, I traced or divined such things; and then in looking at him, I partly understood why, at only about five-and-twenty, Lieutenant Imre von N.....'s forehead showed those three or four lines that were incongruous with as sunny a face. Still, I found enough of the lighter vein in his autobiography to relieve it wholesomely. So I set him down for the average-situated young Hungarian soldier, as to the material side of his life or the rest; blessed with a cheerful temperament and a good appetite, and plagued by no undue faculties of melancholy or introspection. And, by-the-by, merely to hear, to see, Imre von N.... laugh, was to forget that one's own mood a moment earlier had been grave enough. It might be, he had the charm of a child's most infectious mirth, and its current was irresistible.

Now, in remembering what was to come later for us two, I need record here only one incident, in itself slight, of that first afternoon's parliament. I have mentioned that Lieutenant Imre seemed to have his full share of acquaintances, at least of the comrade-class, in Szent Istvánhely. I came to the conclusion as the afternoon went along, that he must be what is known as a distinctly "popular party". One man after another, by no means of only his particular regiment, would stop to chat with him as they entered and quit the garden, or would come over to exchange a bit of chaff with him. And in such of the meetings, came more or less—how shall I call it?—demonstrativeness, never unmanly, which is almost as racial to many Magyarak as to the Italians and Austrians. But afterwards I remembered, as a trait not so much noticed at the time, that Lieutenant Imre, did not seem to be at all a friend of such demeanour. For example, if the interlocutor laid a hand on Lieutenant Imre's shoulder, the Lieutenant quietly drew himself back a little. If a hand were put out, he did not see it at once, nor did he hold it long in the fraternal clasp. It was like a nervous habit of personal reserve; the subtlest sort of mannerism. Yet he was absolutely courteous, even cordial. His regimental friends appeared to meet him in no such merely perfunctory fashion as generally comes from the daily intercourse of the service, the army-world over. One brother-officer paused to reproach him sharply for not appearing at some affair or other at a friend's quarters, on the preceding evening—"when the very cat and dog missed you."

Another comrade wanted to know why he kept "out of a fellow's way, no matter how hard one tries to see something of you." An elderly civilian remained several minutes at his side, to make sure that the young Herr Lieutenant would not forget to dine with the So-and-So family, at a birthday-fête, in course of next few days. Again,— "Seven weeks was I up there, in that d— d little hole in Calizien! And I wrote you long letters, three letters! Not a post-card from you did I get, the whole time!" remonstrated another comrade.

Soon I remarked on this kind of dialogue. "You have plenty of excellent friends in the world, I perceive," said I.

For the first time, that day, since one or another topic had occurred, something like scorn—or a mocking petulance—came across his face.

"I must make you a stale sort of answer, to—pardon me—a very stale little flattery," he answered. "I have acquaintances, many of them quite well enough, as far as they go—men that I see a good deal of, and willingly. But friends? Why, I have the fewest possible! I can count them on one hand! I live too much to myself, in a way, to be more fortunate, even with every Béla, János and Ferencz reckoned-in. I don't believe you have to learn that a man can be always much more alone in his life than appears his case. Much!" He paused and then added:

"And, as it chances, I have just lost, so to say, one of my friends. One of the few of them. One who has all at once gone quite out of my life, as ill-luck would have it. It has given me a downright stroke at my heart. You know how such things affect one. I have been dismal just this very afternoon, absurdly so, merely in realizing it."

"I infer that your friend is not dead?"

"Dead? No, no, not that!" He laughed. "But, all things concerned, he might as well be dead—for me. He is a marine-officer in the Royal Service. We met about four years ago. He has been doing some Government engineering work here. We have been constantly together, day in, day out. Our tastes are precisely the same. For only one of them, he is almost as much a music-fiend as I am! We've never had the least difference. He is the sort of man one never tires of. Everyone likes him! I never knew a finer character, not anyone quite his equal, who could count for as much in my own life. And then, besides," he continued in a more earnest tone, "he is the type to exert on such a fellow, as I happen to be, exactly the influences that are good for me. That I know. A man of iron resolution..... strong will.... energies. Nothing stops him, once he sees what is worth doing, what must be done. Not at all a dreamer.... not morbid.. and so on."

"Well," said I, both touched and amused by this naïveté, "and what has happened?"

"Oh, he was married last month, and ordered to China for time indefinite.... a long affair for the Government. He cannot possibly return for many years, quite likely never."

"Two afflictions at once, indeed," I said, laughing a little, he joining in ruefully. "And might I know under which one of them you, as his deserted Fidus Achates, are suffering most? I infer that you think your friend has added insult to injury."

"What? I don't understand. Ah, you mean the marriage-part of it? Dear me, no! nothing of the sort! I an only too delighted that it has come about for him. His bride has gone out to Hong-Kong with him, and they expect to settle down into the most complete matrimonial bliss there. Besides, she is a woman that I have always admired simply unspeakably... oh, quite platonically, I beg to assure you!.. as have done just about half the men in Szent-Istvánhely, year in and out—who were not as lucky as my friend. She is absolutely charming—of high rank—an old Bohemian family—beautiful, talented, with the best heart in the world..... and-Istenem!" he exclaimed in a sudden, enthusiastic retrospect... "how she sings Brahms! They are the model of a match.... the handsomest couple that you could ever meet."

"Ah... is your marine friend of uncommon good-looks?" He glanced across at the acacia-tree opposite, as if not having heard my careless question, or else as if momentarily abstracted. I was about to make some other remark, when he replied, in an odd, vaguely-directed accent. "I beg your pardon! Oh, yes, indeed... my friend is of exceptional physique. In the service, he is called 'Hermes Karvaly'... his family name is Karvaly.... though there's Sicilian blood in him too—because he looks so astonishingly like that statue you know—the one by that Greek—Praxiteles, isn't it? However, looks are just one detail of Karvaly's unusualness. And to carry out that, never was a man more head over heels in love with his own wife! Karvaly never does anything by halves."

"I beg to compliment on your enthusiasm for your friend... plainly one of the 'real ones' indeed," I said. For, I was not a little stirred by this frank evidence, of a trait that sometimes brings to its possessor about as much melancholy as it does happiness. "Or, perhaps I would better congratulate Mr. Karvaly and his wife on leaving their merits in such generous care. I can understand that this separation means much to you."

He turned full upon me. It was as if he forgot wholly that I was a stranger. He threw back his head slightly, and opened wide those unforgettable eyes—eyes that were, for the instant, sombre, troubled ones.

"Means much? Ah, ah, so very much! I dare say you think it odd.... but I have never had anything... never... work upon me so!.... I couldn't have believed that such a thing could so upset me. I was thinking of some matters that are part of the affair— of its ridiculous effect on me—just when you came here and sat down. I have a letter from him, too, today, with all sorts of messages from himself and his bride, a regular turtle-dove letter. Ah, the lucky people in this world! What a good thing that there are some!" He paused, reflectively. I did not break the silence ensuing. All at once, "Teremtette!" he exclaimed, with a short laugh, of no particular merriment,— "what must you think of me, my dear sir! Pray pardon me! To be talking along—all this personal, sentimental stuff—rubbish—to a perfect stranger! Idiotic!" He frowned irritably, the lines in his brow showing clear. He was looking me in the eyes with a mixture of, shall I say, antagonism and appeal; psychic counter-waves of inward query and of outward resistance.... of apprehension, too. Then, again he said most formally, "I never talked this way with any one—at least never till now. I am an idiot! I beg your pardon."

"You haven't the slightest need to beg it," I answered, "much less to feel the least discomfort in having spoken so warmly of this friendship and separation. Believe me, stranger or not... and, really we seem to be passing quickly out of that degree of acquaintance... I happen to be able to enter thoroughly into your mood. I have a special sense of the beauty and value of friendship. It often seems a lost emotion. Certainly, life is worth living only as we love our friends and are sure of their regard for us. Nobody ever can feel too much of that; and it is, in some respects, a pity that we don't say it out more. It is the best thing in the world, even if the exchange of friendship for friendship is a chemical result often not to be analyzed; and too often not at all equal as an exchange."

He repeated my last phrase slowly, "Too often—not equal!"

"Not by any means. We all have to prove that. Or most of us

do. But that fact must not make too much difference with us; not work too much against our giving our best, even in receiving less than we wish. You may remember that a great French social philosopher has declared that when we love, we are happier in the emotion we feel than in that which we excite."

"That sounds like—like that 'Maxims' gentleman—Rochefoucauld!"

"It was Rochefoucauld."

My vis-à-vis again was mute. Presently he said sharply and with a disagreeable note of laughter, "That isn't true, my dear sir!— that nice little French sentiment! At least I don't believe it is! Perhaps I am not enough of a philosopher—yet. I haven't time to be, though I would be glad to learn how."

With that, he turned the topic. We said no more as to friends, friendship or French philosophy. I was satisfied, however, that my new acquaintance was anything but a cynic, in spite of his dismissal, so cavalierly, of a subject on which he had entered with such abrupt confidentiality.

So had its course my breaking into an acquaintance... no, let me not use as burglarious and vehement a phrase, for we do not take the Kingdom of Friendship by violence even though we are assured that there is that sort of an entrance into the Kingdom of Heaven—so was my passing suddenly into the open door of my intimacy (as it turned out to be) with Lieutenant Imre von N..... It was all as casual as my walking into the Erzsébet-tér Café. That is, if anything is casual. I have set down only a fragment of that first conversation; and I suspect that did I register much more, the personality of Imre would not be significantly sharpened to anyone, that is to say in regard to what was my impression of him then. In what I have jotted, lies one detail of some import; and there is shown enough of the swift confidence, the current of immediate mutuality which sped back and forth between us. "Es gibt ein Zug, ein wunderliches Zug" declares Grillparzer, most truthfully. Such an hour or so.... for the evening was drawing on when we parted..... was a kindly prophecy as to the future of the intimacy, the trust, the decreed progression toward them, even through our—reserves.

We met again, in the same place, at the same hour, a few days later; of course, this time by an appointment carefully and gladly kept. That second evening, I brought him back with me to supper, at the Hotel L——, and it was not until a late hour (for one of the most early-to-bed capitals of Europe) that we bade each other good-night at the restaurant-door. By the by, not till that evening was rectified a minor neglect.... complete ignorance of one another's names! The fourth or fifth day of our ripening partnership, we spent quite and entirely together; beginning it in the same coffee-house at breakfast, making a long inspection of Imre's pleasant lodging, opposite my hotel, and of his music-library; and ending it with a bit of an excursion into one of Szent-Istvánhely's suburbs; and with what had already become a custom, our late supper, with a long aftertalk. The said suppers by the by, were always amusingly modest banquets. Imre was by no means a valiant trencher-man, though so strong-limbed and well-fleshed. So ran the quiet course of our first ten days, our first two weeks, a term in which, no matter what necessary interruptions came, Lieutenant Imre von N.... and I made it clear to one another, though without a dozen words to such effect, that we regarded the time we could pass together as by far the most agreeable, not to say important, matter of each day. We kept on continually adjusting every other concern of the twenty-four hours toward our rendezvous, instinctively. We seemed to have grown so vaguely concerned with the rest of the world, our interests that were not in common now abode in such a curious suppression, they seemed so colourless, that we really appeared to have entered another and a removed sphere inhabited by only ourselves, with each meeting. As it chanced, Imre was for the nonce, free from any routine of duties of a regimental character. As for myself, I had come to Szent-Istvánhely with no set time-limit before me; the less because one of the objects of my stay was studying, under a local professor, that difficult and exquisite tongue which was Imre's native one, though, by the way, he was like so many other Magyars in slighting it by a perverse preference. (For a long time, we spoke only French or German when together.) So between my sense of duty to Magyar, and a sense, even more acute, of a great unwillingness to leave Szent-Istvánhely—it was growing fast to something like an eighth sense... I could abide my time, or the date when Imre must start for certain annual regimental maneuvers, down in Slavonia. With reference to the idle curiosity of our acquaintances as to this so emphatic a state of dualism for Imre and myself.... such an inseparable sort of partnership which might well suggest something...

> *Too rash, too unadvised, too sudden,*
> *Too like the lightening which doth cease to be*
> *Ere one can say 'It lightens'*

Why we were careful. Even in one of the countries of Continental Europe where sudden, romantic friendship is a good deal of a cult, it seems that there is neither wisdom nor pleasure in wearing one's heart on one's sleeve. Best not to placard sudden affinities; between soldiers and civilists, especially. It was Imre von N.... himself who gave me this information, or hint; though not any clear explanation of its need. But he and I not only kept out of the most frequented haunts of social and military Szent-Istvánhely thenceforth, but spoke (on occasion) to others of my having come to the place especially to be with Imre, again,— "for the first time in three years", since we had become "acquainted with each other down in Sarajevo, one morning"— during a visit to the famous Husruf-Beg Mosque there! This easy fabrication was sufficient. Nobody questioned it. As a fact, Imre and I, when comparing notes one afternoon had found out that really we had been in Sarajevo at the exact date mentioned. "The lie that is half a truth is ever".... the safest of lies, as well as the convenientest one.

Now of what did two men thus insistent on one another's companionship, one of them some twenty-five years of age, the other past thirty, neither of them vapourous with the vague enthusiasms of first manhood, nor fluent with the mere sentimentalities of idealism.... of what did we talk, hour in and hour out, that our company was so welcome to each other, even to the point of our being indifferent to all the rest of our friends round about?.... centering ourselves on the time together as the best thing in the world for us. Such a question repeats a common mistake, to begin with. For it presupposes that companionship is a sort of endless conversazione, a State-Council ever in session. Instead, the silences in intimacy stand for the most perfect mutuality. And, besides, no man or woman has yet ciphered out the real secret of the finest quality, clearest sense, of human companionability—a thing that often grows up, flower and fruit, so swiftly as to be like the oriental juggler's magic mango-plant. We are likely to set ourselves to analyzing, over and over, the externals and accidence... the mere inflections of friendships, as it were. But the real secret evades us. It ever will evade. We are drawn together because we are drawn. We are content to abide together just because we are content. We feel that we have reached a certain harbour, after much or little drifting, just because it is for that haven, after all, that we have been moving on and on; with all the irresistible pilotry of the wide ocean-wash friendly to us. It is as foolish to make too much of the definite in friendship as it is in love—which is the highest expression of companionship. Friendship?—love? what are they if real on both sides, but the great Findings? Grillparzer... once more to cite that noble poet of so much that is profoundly psychic... puts all the negative and the positive of it into the appeal of his Jason..

> *In my far home, a fair belief is found,*
> *That double, by the Gods, each human soul*
> *Created is... and, once so shaped, divided.*
> *So shall the other half its fellow seek*
> *O'er land, o'er sea, till when it once be found,*
> *The parted halves, long-sundered, blend and mix*
> *In one, at last! Feel'st thou this half-heart?*
> *Beats it with pain, divided, in thy breast?*
> *O... come!*

As a fact, my new friend and I had an interesting range of commonplace and practical topics, on which to exchange ideas. Sentimentalities were quite in abeyance. We were both interested in art, as well as in sundry of the less popular branches of literature, and in what scientifically underlies practical life. Moreover, I had been longtime enthusiastic as to Hungary and the Hungarians, the land, the race, the magnificent military history, the complicated, troublous aspects of the present and the future of the Magyar Kingdom. And though I cannot deny that I have met with more ardent Magyar patriots than Imre von N... for somehow he took a conservative view of his birth-land and fellow-citizens—still, he was always interested in clarifying my ideas. Again, contrary-wise, Lieutenant Imre was zealous in informing himself on matters and things pertaining to my own country and to its system of social and military life, as well as concerning a great deal more; even to my native language, of which he could speak precisely seven words, four of them too forcible for use in general polite society. Never was there a quicker, a more aggressively intelligent mind than his; the intellect that seeks to take in a thing as swiftly yet as fully as possible.... provided, as Imre confessed, with complete absence of shame, the topic "attracted" him. Fortunately, most interesting topics did so; and what he learned once, he learned for good and all. I smile now as I remember the range, far afield often, of our talks when we were in the mood for one. I think that in those first ten days of our intercourse we touched on, I should say, a hundred subjects—from Árpád the Great to the Seventh Symphony, from the prospects of the Ausgleich to the theory of Bisexual Languages, from Washington to Kossuth, from the novels of Jókai to the best gulyás, from harvesting-machines, drainage, income-taxes, and whether a woman ought to wear earrings or not, to the Future State! No,—one never was at a loss for a topic when with Imre, and one never tired of his talk about it, any more than one tired of Imre when mute as Memnon, because of his own meditations, or when he was, apparently, like the Jolly Young Waterman, "rowing along, thinking of nothing at all."

And besides more general matters, there was... for so is it in friendship as in love... ever that quiet undercurrent of inexhaustible curiosity about each other as an Ego, a psychic fact not yet mutually explained. Therewith comes in that kindly seeking to know better and better the Other, as a being not yet fully outlined, as one whom we would understand even from the farthest-away time when neither friend suspected the other's existence, when each was meeting the world alone—as one now looks back on those days... and was absorbed in so much else in life, before Time had been willing to say, "Now meet, you two! Have I not been preparing you for each other?" So met, the simple personal retrospect is an ever new affair of detail for them, with its queries, its concessions, its comparisons. "I thought that, but now I think this. Once on a time I believed that, but now I believe this. I did so and so, in those old days; but now, not so. I have desired, hoped, feared, purposed, such or such a matter then; now no longer. Such manner of man have I been, whereas nowadays my identity before myself is thus and so." Or, it is the presenting of what has been enduringly a part of ourselves, and is likely ever abide such? Ah, these are the moods and tenses of the heart and the soul in friendship! more and more willingly uttered and listened-to as intimacy and confidence thrive. Two natures are seeking to blend. Each is glad to be its own directory for the newcomer; to treat him as an expected and welcomed guest to the Castle of Self, while yet something of a stranger to it; opening to him any doors and windows that will throw light on the labyrinth of rooms and corridors, wishing to keep none shut.... perhaps not even some specially haunted, remote and even black-hung chamber. Guest? No, more than that, for is it not the tenant of all others, the Master, who at last, has arrived!

Probably this is the best place in my narrative to record certain particularly personal aspects of Lieutenant Imre, though in giving them I must draw on details and impressions that I gained gradually—later. During even that earlier stage of our friendship, he insisted on my going with him to his father's house, to meet his parents. From them, as from two or three of his officer-friends with whom I occasionally foregathered, when Imre did not happen to be of the party of us, I derived facts—side-lights and perspectives—of use. But the most part of what I note came from Imre's tendency toward introspection; and from his own frank lips.

He had been a singularly sensitive, warm-hearted boy, indeed too high-strung, too impressionable. He had been petted by even the merest strangers because of his engaging manners and his peculiarly striking boyish beauty. He had not been robust as a lad (though now superbly so) with the result that his schooling had been desultory and unsystematic. "And I wanted to study art, I didn't care what art... music, painting, sculpture, perhaps music more than anything... I hated the army! But my father—his heart was set on my doing what the rest of us had done... I was the only son left.. it had to be." And however little was Imre at heart a soldier, he had made himself into a most excellent officer. I soon heard that from all his comrades whom I met; and I have heard it often since those days in Szent-Istvánhely. His sense of his personal duty, his pride, his filial affection, his feeling toward his King, all contributed toward the outward semblance that was at least so desirable. He had already been highly commended; probably promotion would soon come. He had always won cordial words from his superiors. Loving not in the least the work, he played his unwelcome part well and manly, so that not more than half a dozen individuals could have been sure that Imre von N... hadnagy, would have doffed gladly, at any minute, the King's Coat for a blouse. Ambition failed him, alas! just because he was at heart indifferent to the reward. But he ran the race well. And for the matter of ambition the advancement in the Magyar service is as deliberate as in other armies in peace-times. Imre needed much stronger influence than what was at his request, to hurry him beyond a lieutenancy.

With only one such contest in his soul, no wonder that Imre led his life in Szent-Istvánhely so much to himself, however open to others it seemed to be. Yet whatever depressed him, he was determined not to be a man of moods to the cynical world's eyes. As a fact he was so happily a creature of buoyant temperament, that his popularity was not surprising, on the basis of comrade-intercourse and of the pleasantly superficial side of a regimental life. Every man was Imre's friend! Every woman was, such, that I ever heard speaking of him, or spoken-of along with his name. The paradox of living to oneself while living with everyone, the doors of an individuality both open and shut, could no farther go than in his instance.

How fully was I to realize that, in a little time!

As to physique, Imre had fulfilled in his maturity the promise of his boyhood. He was called "Handsome N...", right and left; and he deserved the sobriquet. Of middle height, he possessed a slender figure, faultless in proportions, a wonder of muscular development, of strength, lightness and elegance. His athletic powers were renowned in his regiment. He was among the crack gymnasts, vaulters and swimmers. I have seen him, often, make a standing-leap over an ordinary library-table, to land, like a cat, on the other side. I have seen him, half-a-dozen times, spring out of a common barrel into another one placed beside it, without touching his hands to either. He could hold out a heavy garden-chair perfectly straight, with one hand; break a stout penholder or leadpencil between his second and third fingers; and bend a thick, brass curtain-rod by his leg-muscles. He frequently swam directly across the wide Duna, making nothing of its cross-currents at Szent-Istvánhely. He was a consummate fencer, and a prize-shot. He could jump on and off a running horse, like a vaquero. Yet all this force, this muscular address, was concealed by the symmetry of his graceful, elastic frame. Not till he was nude, and one could trace the ripple of muscle and sinew under the fine, hairless skin, did one realize the machinery of such strength. I have never seen any other man—unless Magyar, Italian or Arab—walk with such elasticity and dignity. It was a pleasure simply to see Imre cross the street.

His head, a small, admirably shaped one, with its close-cut golden hair, carried out his Hellenic exterior. For it was really a small head to be set on such broad shoulders and on as well-grown a figure. As to his face (generally a detail of least relative importance in the male type), I do not intend to analyze retrospectively certainly one of the most engaging of manly countenances that I have ever looked upon. The actual features were delicate enough, but without womanishness. Imre was not a pretty man; but a beautiful man. And the mixture of maturity and of almost boyish youth, the outlook of his natural sincerity and warmth of nature, his self-unconsciousness and self-respect... these entered into the matter of his good looks, quite as much as his merely technical beauty. I did not wonder that not only the women in Szent-Istvánhely but the street-children, aye, the very dogs and cats it seemed to me, would look at him with friendly interest. Those lustrous hazel eyes, with the white so clear around the pupils... the indwelling laughter in them that nevertheless could be overcast with so penetrating a seriousness...! It seems to me that now, as I write, I meet their look. I lay down my pen for an instant as my own eyes suddenly blur. Yet why? We should find tears rising for a living grief, not a living joy!

United with all this capital of a man's physical attractiveness was Imre's extraordinary modesty. He never seemed to think of his appearance for so much as two minutes together. He never glanced into a mirror when he happened to pass near that piece of furniture which seems to inflict a sort of nervous disease of the eyes... occasionally also of the imagination... on the average soldier of any rank and uniform, the world round. "Thanks... but I don't trouble myself much about looking-glasses, when I've once got my clothes on my back and am certain that my face isn't dirty!" was his reply to me one morning when I gave him an amused look because he had happened to plant his chair exactly in front of the biggest pier-glass in the K... Café. He never posed; never fussed as to his toilet, nor worried concerning the ultrafitting of his clothes, nor studied with anxiety details of his person. One day, another officer was lamenting the melancholy fact that baldness was gaining ground slyly, pitilessly, on the speaker's hyacinthine locks. He gave utterance to a sorrowful envy of Imre. "Pooh, pooh," returned Imre, hadnagy, scornfully, "It's in the family... and such a convenience in warm weather! I shall be bald as a cannon-shot by the time I am thirty!" He detested all jewellery in the way of masculine adornments, and wore none: and his civilian clothing was of the plainest.

The making-up of every man refers, or should do so, to a fourfold development... his physical, mental, moral and temperamental equipment, in which last-named class we can include the aesthetic individuality. The endowment of Imre von N... as to this series was decidedly less symmetrical than otherwise. In fact, he was a striking example of contradictions and inequations. He had studied hardest when in his school-courses just what came easiest... with the accustomed results of that sort of process. He was a bad, a perversely bad mathematician; an indifferent linguist, simply because he had found it "a hideous job to learn all those complicated verbs"; an excellent scholar in history; took delight in chemistry and in other physical sciences; and though so easily plagued by a simple sum in decimals, he had a passion for astronomy, and he knew not a little about it, at least theoretically. Physical science appealed to him, curiously; his small library was two-thirds full of books on those topics. He loved to read popular philosophy and biography and travel. For novels, as for poetry, he cared almost nothing. He would spare no pains to get to the bottom of some subject that interested him, a thing that "bit" him, as he called it; short of actually setting himself down to the calm and applicative study of it! Tactics did he, somehow deliberately learn; grimly, angrily, but with success. They were indispensable to his professional credit. Such a result showed plainly enough that he lacked resolution, concentration as a duty, but did not lack capability. Many a sound lecture from myself, as from other friends, including particularly, as I found out, from the much-married Karvaly, did Imre receive respecting this defect. A course in training in the Officers' Military School (Hadiskola) was involved in the difficulty, or perversity, so in evidence. This Hadiskola course is an indispensable in such careers as Imre's sort should achieve, willing or unwilling. When a young officer is so obstinately cold to what lies toward good work in the Hadiskola, and in his inmost soul desires almost anything rather than becoming even an major... why, what can one say severe enough to him?

Yet, with reference to what might be called Imre's aesthetic self-expression, I wish to record one thing at variance with much which was negative in him. At least it was in contradiction to his showing such modest "literary impulses", and to his relative aversion to belles-lettres, and so on. When Imre was deeply stirred over something or other that "struck home", by some question to open the mountains of innermost feeling in him, it was remarkable with what exactitude,—more than that, what genuine emotional eloquence of phrase—he could express himself! This even to losing that slight hesitancy of diction which was an ordinary characteristic. I was often surprised at the simple, direct beauty, sometimes downright poetic grace, in his language on such unexpected occasions. He seemed to become tinged with quite another personality, or to be following, in a kind of trance, the prompting of some voice audible to him only. I shall hardly so much as once attempt conveying this effect of sudden "ihletés", even in coming to the moments of our intercourse when it surged up. It must in most part be taken for granted; read between the lines now and then. But... one must be mindful of its natural explanation. For, after all, there was no miracle in it. Imre was a Magyar; one of a race in which sentimental eloquence is always lurking in the blood, even to a poetic passion in verbal utterance that is often out of all measure with the mere formal education of a man or a woman. He was a Hungarian: which means among other things that a cowherd who cannot write his name, and who does not know where London is, can be overheard making love to his sweetheart, or lamenting the loss of his mother, in language that is almost of Homeric beauty. It is the Oriental quality, ever in the Magyar; now to be admired by us, now disliked, according to the application of the traits. Imre had his full share of Magyarism of temperament, and of its impromptu eloquence; taking the place of much of a literal acquaintance with Dante, Shakespeare, Goethe, and all the rhetorical and literary Parnassus in general.

He detested politics, as might be divined. He "loved" his Apostolic King and his country much as do some children their nearest relatives; that is to say, on general principles, and to the sustaining of a correct attitude before himself and the world. On this matter, also he and I had many passages-at-arms. He had not much "religion." But he was a firm believer in God; in helping one's neighbour, even to most injudicious generosity; in avoiding debts "when one could possibly do so" (a reserve that I regretted to find out was not his case any more than it is usually the case with young Hungarian officers living in a capital city, with small home-subventions); in honour; in womanly virtue; in a true tongue and a clean one. His sense of fun was not limited to the kind that may pass between a rector of the Establishment and his daughters over afternoon-tea. But Lieutenant Imre von N.... had no relish for the stupid-smutty sallies and stock racontars of the officers' mess and the barracks. Unless a "story" really possessed wit and humour, he had absolutely dull ears for it.

He wrote a shameful handwriting, with invariable hurry-scurry; he could not draw a pot-hook straight, and he took uncertain because untaught interest in painting. Sculpture, and architecture appealed more to him, though also in an untaught way. But he was a most excellent practical musician; playing the piano-forte superbly well, as to general effect, with an amazingly bad technic of his own evolution, got together without any teaching; and not reading well and rapidly at sight. Indeed, his musical enthusiasm, his musical insight and memory, they were all of a piece; the rich and perilous endowment of the born son of Orpheus. His singing-voice was a full baritone.... smooth and sweet, like his irresistible speaking-voice. He would play or sing for hours together, quite alone in his rooms, of an evening. He would go without his dinner (he often did) to pay for his concert-ticket or standing-place in the Royal Opera. He did not care for the society of professional musicians, or of the theaterfolk in general. "They really are not worth while," he used to say... "art is one thing to me and artists another—or nothing at all—off the stage." As for more general society, why, he said frankly that nowadays the N.... family simply were too poor to go into it, and that he had no time for it. So he was to be met in only a few of the Szent-Istvánhely drawing rooms. Yet he was passionately fond of dancing.... anything from a waltz to a csárdás. But, à-propos of Imre's amusement, let me note here (for I dare say, the incredulity of persons who have stock-ideas of what belongs to soldier-life and soldier-nature) that three usual pleasures were not his; for he abominated cards, indeed never played them; he did not smoke; and he seldom drank out his glass of wine or beer, having no taste for liquors of any sort. This in a champion athlete and an "all-round" active soldier... at least externally thoroughly such... in a smart regiment, is not common. I should have mentioned above that he was oddly indifferent to the theater, as the theater; declaring that he never could find "any great illusion" in it. He much liked billiards, and was invincible in them. His feeling for whatever was natural, simple, out-of-doors was great. He loved to walk, to walk alone, in the open country, in the woodlands and fields... to talk with peasants, who invariably "took to" him at once. He loved children, and was a born animal-friend; in fact, between him and beasts little and big, there appeared to be a regular understanding. Never forthputting, he could delight, in a quiet way in the liveliest company. That buoyancy of his temperament, so in contrast with the other elements of his nature, was a vast blessing to him. He certainly had a supply of personal subjects sufficiently sobering for home-consumption, some of which I soon knew; others not spoken till later. The gloom in his parents' house, the various might-have-beens in his own young life, the wearisome struggle to do his duty in a professional career whereto he had been called without its being chosen by him; weightier still the fact that he was in the hands of a couple of usurers on account of his generous share of the deficit in a foolish brother officer's finances, to the extent of some thousands of florins.... these were not trifles for Imre's private meditations. I could quite well understand his remarking... "I have tried to cultivate cheerfulness on just about the same principle that when a man hasn't a korona in his pocket he does well to dress himself in his best clothes and swagger in the Officers' Casino as if he were a millionaire. For the time, he forgets that he isn't one... poor devil!"

But I am belated, I see, in alluding to two traits in our acquaintance, ab initio, which are of significance in my outline of Imre's personality while new to me: and more than trifles in their weight. There were two subjects as to which remarkably little was said between us during the first ten days of my going-about so much with him. "Remarkably little" I say, because of Imre's own frank references to one matter, on our first meeting; and because we were both men, and neither of us octogenarians, nor troubled with super-sensitiveness in talking about all sorts of things. The first of these overpassed topics was the friendship between Imre and the absent Karvaly Miklos. Since the afternoon on which we had met, Imre referred so little to Karvaly.... he seemed so indifferent to his absence, all at once... indeed he appeared to be shunning the topic... that I avoided it completely. It gradually was borne in upon me that he wished me to avoid it. So no more expansiveness on the perfections and gifts of the exile! Of Karvaly's young bride, on the other hand, the fascinating Bohemian lady who sang Brahms' songs so beautifully, Imre was still distinctly eloquent; alluding often to one or another of her shining attributes... paragon that she may have been! I write 'may have been'; because to this day I know her, like Shakespeare's Olivia,— "only by her good report".

The other matter of our reticence was an instance of the difference between the general and the particular. Very early in my meeting with Imre's more immediate circle of soldier-friends, I heard over and over again that to Imre, as one of the officers most distinguished in all the town for personal beauty, there attached a reputation of being an ever-campaigning and ever-victorious Don Juan... if withal one of most exceptional discretion. Right and left, he was referred to as a wholesale enemy to the peace of heart and to the virtue of dozens of the fair citizenesses of Szent-Istvánhely. Two of these romances, the heroine of one of them being an extremely beautiful and refined déclassée whose sudden suicide had been the gossip of the clubs, were heightened by the touch of the tragic. But along with them, and the more ordinary chatter about a young man's bonnes fortunes, or what were taken to be them, there were surmises and assertions of vague, aristocratic, deep, unconfessed ties and adventures. The Germans use the terms "Weiberfreund" and "Weiberfeind" in rather a special sense sometimes. Now, I knew that Imre von N... was no woman-hater. He admired, and had a circle of admiring, women-friends enough to dismiss at once such an ungallant accusation. Never was there a sharper eye, not even in Magyarország, for an harmonious female figure, a graceful carriage, a charming face.... he was a connaisseur de race!

But when it came to his alluding, when we were by ourselves, to anything like really intimate sentimental—I would best plainly say amorous—relations with the other sex, Imre never opened his mouth for a word of the least real significance! He referred to himself, casually, now and then, and as it appeared to me in precisely the right key, as one to whom woman was a sufficiently definite social and physical attraction.... necessity... quite as essentially as is to be expected with a young soldier of normal health and robust constitution. When it suited his mixed society, he had as many "discreet stories" as Poins. But when he and I were alone, no matter whatever else he spoke of... so unreservedly, so temperamentally!—he never did what is commonly called "talk women." He never so much alluded to a light-o' love, to an "affair", to any distinctly sexual interest in a ballerina or—a princess! And when third parties were pleased to compliment him, or to question him, as to such a thing, Imre "smiling put the question by." His special reserve concerning these topics, so rare in men of his profession and age, was as emphatic as in the instance of the average English gentleman. I admired it, certainly not wishing it less. I often thought how well it became Imre's general refinement of disposition, manners and temperamental bias... most of all, suiting that surprising want of vanity as to his person, his character, his entire individuality.

In this connection, came a bit of an incident that has its significance... as things came to pass later in our acquaintance.

One evening, while I was dressing for dinner, with Imre making a random visit, I lapsed into hearty irritation as to a marvellously ill-fitting new garment, that was to be worn for the first time. Imre was pleased to be facetious. "You ought to go into the tailoring-line yourself," he observed... "then you can adorn yourself as perfectly as you would wish!" I threw out some sort of a return-banter that his own carelessness as to his looks was "the pride that apes humility."

"One would really suppose," I remarked, "that you do not know why a pretty woman makes eyes at you!... Are you under the impression that you are admired on account of the Three Christian Graces and the Four Theological Virtues?—all on sight! Come now, my dear fellow, you really need not carry the pose so far!"

Imre opened his lips as if about to say something or other; and then made no remark. Once more he gave me the idea that he was minded to speak, but hesitated. So I suspended operations with my hairbrushes.

"You appear to be labouring with a remarkably difficult idea," I said.

He answered abruptly: "There are some things it is hard for a man to judge of, even in another fellow... at least people say so. See here, you! I wish... I wish you would tell me something.... you won't think me a conceited ass? Do you... for instance... do you... find me really specially good-looking... when you look around the lot of other men one sees.... in comparison with plenty of others, I mean?"

"Do you want an answer in chaff, or seriously?"

"Seriously."

"I most certainly think you 'specially' such, N...."

"And you are of the opinion that most people... women... men... sculptors, for instance, or painters..: a photographer, if you like.... ought to be of your opinion?"

"But yes, assuredly," I replied, laughing at what seemed the naiveté and uncalled-for earnestness in his tone. "You do not need to put me on oath, such a newcomer, too, into your society, to give you the conviction. Or, stay... how would you like me to draft you a kind of technical schedule, my dear fellow, stating how and why you are—not repulsive? I could give it to you, if I thought it would be good for you, and if you would listen to it. For you are one of those lucky ones in the world whose good-looks can be demonstrated, categorically, so to say—trait by trait—passport-style. Come, come, N——! Don't be so depressed because you are so beautiful! Cheer up! Probably there will always be somebody in the wide world who will not care to bestow even an half-eye on you!... some being who remains, first and last, totally unimpressed, brutally unmoved, by all your manly charms! I dare say that if you consult that individual you will be assured that you are the most ordinary-looking creature in creation."

As I spoke, Imre who had been sitting, three-quarters turned from me, over at a window, whisked himself about quickly and gave me what I thought was a most inexplicable look. "Have I offended him?" I asked myself; ridiculous to me, even at so early a stage of our intimacy, as was the notion. But I saw that his look was not one of surprised irritation. It was not one of dissent. He continued looking at me... ah, his serious eyes!... whatever else he was seeing in his perturbed mind.

"Well," I continued, "isn't that probable? Have I made you angry by hinting at such a stupidity.... such an aesthetic tragedy?"

"No, no," he returned hastily,— "of course not!" And then with a laugh as curious as that look of his, for it was not his real, his cheerful and heart-glad laugh, but one that rang false even to being ill-humored, he added... "By God, you have spoken the truth! Yes, to the dot on the i!"

I did not pursue the subject. I saw that it was one, whatever else was part of it, that was better left for Imre himself to take up at some other time; or not at all. Apparently, I had stumbled on one little romance; possibly on a grande passion! In either case it was a matter not dead, if moribund it might be. Imre could open himself to me thereon, or not: I was not curious, nor a purveyor of reading-matter to fashionable London journals.

Two matters more in this diagnosis... shall I call it so?... of my friend. Let me rather say that it is a memorandum and guidebook of Imre's emotional topography.

Something has been said of the spontaneous warmth of his temperament, and of his enthusiasm for his closer friends. But his undemonstrativeness also mentioned, seemed to me more and more curiously accentuated. Imre might have been an Englishman, if it came to outward signs of his innermost feelings. He neither embraced, kissed, caressed nor what else his friends; and, as I had surmised, when first being with him and them, he did not appear to like what in his part of the world are ordinary degrees of "demonstrativeness". He never invited nor returned (to speak as Brutus)— "the shows of love in other men". There was a certain captain in the A.... Regiment, a man that Imre much liked and, what is more, had more than once admired in good set terms, when with me. ("He is as beautiful as a statue, I think!") This brother-soldier being suddenly returned to Szent-Istvánhely, after a couple of years of absence, hurried up to Imre and fairly threw his arms about him. Imre was cordiality itself. But after Captain R.... had left him, Imre made a wry face at me, and said... "The best fellow in the world! and generally speaking, most rational! But I do wish he had forgotten to kiss men! It is so hideously womanish!" Another time we were talking of letters between intimate friends. "I hate... I absolutely hate... to write letters, even to my nearest friends", he protested, "in fact, I never write unless there is no getting-out of it! Five words on a post-card, once a month or so... two or three months, maybe... and lucky if they get that! How do I write? Something like this... 'I am here and well. How are you. We are very busy. I saw your cousin, Csodaszép Kisasszony yesterday. No time to-day for more! Kindest regards. Alá szolgája! N....'. Now there you have my style to a dot. What more in the world is really called-for? As for sentiment... sentiment! in letters to my friends!... well, I simply cannot squeeze that out, or in. Nobody need expect it from your most obedient servant! My correspondence is like telegrams."

"Thanks much," I returned, smiling, "your remarks are most timely, considering that you and I have agreed to keep in touch with each other by post, after I leave here. Forewarned is forearmed! Might I ask, by the by, whether you are as laconic in writing, to—say, your friend Karvaly, over there in China? And if he is satisfied?"

"Karvaly? Certainly. He happens to like precisely that sort of communications particularly well. I never give him ten words where five will do." To which statement I retorted that it was a vast blessing that some persons were easily pleased, as well as so likeminded; and that perhaps it would be quite as wise under such conditions, not to write at all; except maybe on All-Souls Day!

"Perhaps," assented Imre.

So much, then, of your outward individuality and environment, with somewhat of your inner self, my dear Imre!... chiefly as I looked upon you and strove to sum you up during those first days. But was there not one thing more, one most special point of personal interest?... of peculiar solicitude?.. one supreme undercurrent of query and wondering in my mind, as we were thus thrown together, and as I felt my thoughts more and more busied with what was our mutual liking and instinctive trust? Surely there was! I should find myself turning aside from the path of straightest truth which I would hold-to in these pages, if I did not find that question written down early and frankly here, with the rest. It must be written, or be this record broken now and here!

Was Imre von N... what is called among psychiaters of our day, an homosexual? an Urning?—in his instincts and feelings and life?—in his psychic and physical attitude toward women and men? Was he an Uranian? Or was he sexually entirely normal and Dionian? Or, a blend of the two types, a Dionian-Uranian? Or what,... or what not? For that something of a special sexual attitude, hidden, instinctive, was maintained by him, no matter what might be the outward conduct of his life—this I could not help believing, at least at times.

Uranian? Similisexual? Homosexual? Dionian?

Profound and often all too oppressive, even terrible, can be the significance of those cold psychic-sexual terms to the man who.... "knows." To the man who "knows!" Even more terrible to those who understand them not, may be the human natures of which they are but new and clumsy technical symbols, the mere labels of psychiatric study, within a few decades of medical explorers.

What, then, was my new friend?

I could not determine! The more I reflected, the less I perceived. It is so easy to be deceived by just such a mingling of psychic and physic and temperamental traits; easy to dismiss too readily the counterbalancing qualities. I had learned that much. Long before now, I had found it out as a practical psychiater, in my own interests and necessities, by painful experience. Precisely how suggestive, and yet how adverse... where quite vaguely?.. where with a fairly clear accent?.. was inference in Imre's case to be drawn or thrown aside, those who are intelligent in the subtle problems of Uranianism or its absence, can appreciate best. I had been a good deal struck with the passionate—as it seemed—note in Imre's friendship for the absentee, Karvaly Mihály. I noticed the dominance that men, simply as men, seemed to maintain in Imre's daily life and ideals. I studied his reserved relations toward the other sex; the general scope of his tastes, likes and dislikes, his emotional constitution. But all these suffice not to prove... to prove... the deeply-buried mystery of a heart's uranistic impulses, the mingling in the firm, manly nature of another inborn sexual essence which can be mercifully dormant; or can wax unquiet even to a whole life's unbroken anguish!...

And, after all, why should I... I... seek to drag out from him such a secret of his individuality? Was that for me? Hardly, even if I, probably, of all those who now stood near to Imre von N.... But there! I had no right! Even if I..... But there! I swore to myself that I had no wish!

It was Imre himself who gave me a sort of determinative, just as—after the oaths at which love laughs—I was querying with myself what I might do believe.

One evening, we were walking home, after an hour or so with his father and mother. As we turned the corner of a certain brilliantly-lighted café, a man of perhaps forty years, with the unmistakeable suggestion of a soldier about him, and of much distinction of person along with it, but in civilian's dress, came out and passed us. He looked at Imre as if almost startled. Then he bowed. Imre returned his salutation with so particular a coldness, an immediate change of expression, that I noticed it.

"Who is he?" I asked. "Somehow I fancy he is not in your best books."

"No, I can't say that he is," responded Imre. After a moment of silence he went on. "That gentleman used to be a captain in our regiment. He was asked to leave the service. So he left it— about three years ago."

"Why?"

"On account of..." here Imre's voice took on a most disagreeable sneer.. "of a little love-affair."

"Really? Since when was a little love-affair a topic for the action of a regimental Ehrenrath?"

"It happened to be his little love-affair with a.... cadet. You understand?"

"Ah, yes, now I understand. A great scandal, I presume?"

"Scarcely any at all. In fact, nobody, to this day, knows how far the... intimacy really went. But gradually some sort of a story got about... as to the discovery of "relations"... perhaps really amounting to only a trifling incident... But, the man's character was smirched. The regiment's Council didn't go into details... didn't even ask for the facts. He simply was requested privately to give up his charge. You know, or perhaps you do not know, how specially sensitive... indeed implacable.. the Service is on that topic. Anything but a hint of it! There mustn't be a suspicion, a breath! One is simply ruined!"

I stopped to pay our tolls for the long Suspension Bridge. As we pursued our walk, Imre said:

"Do you have any such affairs in England?"

"Yes. Certainly."

"In military life?"

"In military and civil life. In every kind of life."

"Indeed. And.. how do you understand that sort of thing?"

"What sort of thing?"

"A... a man's feeling that way for another man? What's the explanation?—the excuse for it?"

"Oh, I don't pretend to understand it. There are things we would better not try to understand..."

Ah, had I only finished that the sentence as I certainly meant to do in beginning it!... with some such words as "—so much as often to pardon." But the sentence remained open; and I know that it sounded as if it was meant to end with some such phrase as "... because they are so beyond any understanding, beyond any excuse!"

Imre walked on beside me, whistling softly. Just two or three notes, over and over, no tune. Then he remarked abruptly:

"Did you ever happen to meet with... that sort of a man... person... yourself... in your own circle of friends?"

Again the small detail, this time one of commission, not omission, on my part! Through it this narrative is, I suspect, twice as long as otherwise it would have been. "Did I ever know such a man... a 'person'... in my own circle of friends?" Irony could no farther go! I laughed, not in mirth, not in contempt, but in sheer bitterness of retrospect. There are instants when it may be said of other men than Cassius:

And when he smiles, he smiles in such a sort
As if he mocked himself...

Yes, I laughed. And unfortunately Imre von N... thought that I sneered; that I sneered at my fellow-men!

"Yes," I replied, "I knew such a man, such a 'person.' On the whole, pretty well. He had other rather acceptable qualities, you see; so I didn't allow myself to be too much stirred up by... that remarkably queer one."

"Lately?" Imre asked.

"Oh, yes, very lately," I returned flippantly.

Imre spoke no word for several steps. Then, hesitatingly...

"Perhaps you didn't know him quite as thoroughly as you supposed. Were you quite sure?"

"Quite sure." Then, sharply in another sentence that was uttered on impulse and with more of the equivocal in it which afterward I understood, I added, "I think we will not talk any more about him: I mean in that respect... Imre."

Again silence. One-two, one-two—on we went, step and step, over the resonant, deserted bridge. I had an impression that Imre turned his head, looking sharply at me in the fluttering gas-light... then glancing quickly away. I had other thoughts, far, far removed from him! I had well-nigh forgot when I was!—forgot him, forgot Szent-Istvánhely........!

But now he laughed out, too, as if in angry derision.

"I say! I knew such a fellow, too.. two or three years ago. And I beg to tell you that he fell in love with.. me! No less! He was absolutely bódult over your humble servant. Did you ever!"

"Really? What did you do? Slap his face, and give him the address of a... doctor of nervous diseases?"

"Oh, Lord, no! I merely declined with thanks the.... honour of his farther acquaintance. I told him never to speak me. He left town. I had rather liked him. But I heard he had been compromised already. I have no use for that particular brand of fool!"

Are there perverse demons, demons delighting to make mortal men blunderers in simplest word and action... that haunt the breezy Lánczhíd in Szent-Istvánhely? If so, some of us would better cross that long bridge in haste and solitary silence after nightfall. For:

"You surprise me," I said lightly. I was thinking of one of his own jests as well of his unbelief in his personal attractions. "How inconsistent for you! Now you are just the very individual I should suspect!...... yes, yes, I am surprised!"

To my astonishment, Imre stopped full in his steps, drew himself up, and faced me with instant formality.

"Will you be so good as to tell me why you are surprised?" asked he, in a tone that was—I will not write sharp, but which suggested to me immediately that I had spoken mal-à-propos or misleadingly; the more so in view of what Imre had mentioned of his ex professio and personal sensitiveness to the general topic. "Do you observe anything particularly womanish—abnormal—about me, if you please?"

Now, as it happened my remark, as I have said, was made in consequence of an impersonal and amusing incident, which I had supposed Imre would at once remember.

"Womanish? Abnormal? Certainly not. But you seem to forget what you yourself said to Captain Molten this afternoon... in the billiard-room... about the menage-cooks... don't you remember?"

Imre burst into laughter. He remembered! (There is no need of my writing out here a piece of humour not transferable with the least esprit into English, though mighty funny in Magyar.) His mood changed at once. He took my arm, a rare attention from him, and we said no more till the Bridge was past, and the corner which divided our lodgings by a street's breadth was reached. We said "Good-night!... till tomorrow!"... the házmester opened his door. Imre waved his hand gaily and vanished.

I got to bed, concluding among other things that so far from Imre's being homosexual—as Uranian, or Dionian-Uranian, or Uranian-Dionian... or what else of that kind of juggling terminology in homosexual analysis—my friend was no sort of an Uranistic example at all. No! he was, instead, a thorough-going Dionian, whatever the fine fusions of his sensitive and complex nature! A complete Dionian, capable of warm friendship, yes—but a man to whom warm, even passionate, friendship with this or that other man never could transform itself into the bitter and burning mystery of Uranistic Love,—the fittest names for which so often should be written Torment, Shame, and Despair!

Fortunate Imre! Yet, as I said so to myself, altruistically glad for his sake, I sighed... and surely that night I thought long, long thoughts till I finally slept.

II. MASKS AND—A FACE

My whole life was a contest since the day
That gave me being, gave me that which marred
The gift....
A silent suffering and intense....
All that the proud can feel of pain,
The agony they do not show....
Which speaks it in its loneliness.
— BYRON

A couple of miles out of Szent-Istvánhely, one finds the fine old seat, or what was such, of the Z... family, with its deserted chateau and neglected park. The family is a broken and dispersed one. The present owner of the premises lives in Paris. He visits them no oftener, and spends no more for their care than he cannot help. The park itself is almost a forest, so large it is and so stately are the trees. Long, wide alleys wind through the acacias and chestnuts. You do not go far from the very house without hares running by you, and partridges and pheasant fluttering; so left to itself is the whole demesne. Like most old estates near Szent-Istvánhely, it has its legends, plentifully. One of these tales, going back to the days of the Turkish sieges of the city, tells how a certain Count Z..., a young soldier of only twenty-six years, during the investment of 1565, was sitting at dinner, in the citadel, when word was brought that a Turkish skirmishing-party had captured his cousin, to whom he was deeply attached; and had cruelly murdered the young man here, in the park of this same chateau, which during some days the lines of the enemy had approached. The officer sprang up from the table. He held up his sword, and swore by it, and Saint Stephen of Hungary, that he would not put the sword back into its sheath, nor sit down to a table, nor lie in a bed, till he had avenged his cousin's fate. He collected a little troop—in an hour. Before another one had passed, he made a sortie, under a pretext, toward his invaded estate. He forced its defences. He drove out the enemy's post. He found and buried his cousin's mutilated body. Then, before dawn, he himself was surprised by a fresh force of Turks. He was shot, standing by his friend's grave... in which he too eventually was buried. Their monument is there to-day, with the story on it, beginning: "To The Unforgettable Memory of Z... Lorand, and Z... Egon", after the customary Magyar name-inversion.

The public was not admitted to this old bit of the Szent-Istvánhely suburbs. But persons known to the caretakers were welcome. Lieutenant Imre and I had been out there once before, with the more freedom because a certain family-connection existed between the Z—s and the N—s. So was it that about a week after the little incident closing the preceding portion of this narrative, we planned to go out to Z.... for the end of the afternoon. A suburban electric tramway passed near the gates.

For two days, I had been superstitiously.... absurdly... irresistibly oppressed with the idea that some disagreeable thing was coming my way. We all have such fits; sometimes justifiably, if often, thank Heaven! proving them quite groundless. I had laughed at mine, with Imre. I could think of no earthly reason for expecting ill to befall me. To myself, I accounted for the mood as a simple reaction of temperament. For, I had been extremely happy lately; and now there was the ebb, not of the happiness, but of the hyper-sensitiveness to it all. The balance would presently be found, and I would be neither too glad nor too gloomy.

"But why.. why... have you found yourself so wonderfully happy lately?" had asked Imre, curiously. "You haven't inherited a million? Nor fallen in love?"

No—I had not inherited a million.......

It was on my way to the tram, to meet Imre, that same afternoon, that I found, from my letters from England, why justly I should exclaim:

> *My soul hath felt a secret weight,*
> *A warning of approaching fate....*

I was wanted in London within four days! I must start within less than twenty-four hours! A near relative was in uncertainty and anxiety as to some special personal affairs. And not only was my entire programme for the next few weeks completely broken up; worse still, was a strong probability that I might be hindered from setting foot on the Continent for indefinite time. In any case, a return to Hungary under less than a full twelvemonth was not now to be thought-of.

With this fall of the proverbial bolt out of a clear sky, in the shape of that letter in my pocket, from Onslow Square, I hurried toward the tram and Imre. All my pleasure in the afternoon and in everything else was paralyzed. Astonishing was it how heavy-hearted I had become in course of glancing through that communication from Mrs L..., between the Ipar-Bank and the street-corner.

Heavy-hearted? Yes, miserably heavy-hearted!...

Why so? Was it because of the worriments of Mrs. L...? Because I could not loiter, as a travelling idler, in pleasant Szent-Istvánhely?—could not go on studying Magyar there; and anon set out for the Herkules-Baths? Hardly any of these were good and sufficient reasons for suddenly feeling as if life were not worth living! that a world where departings, and partings along with them, seemed to be the main reason for one's comings and meetings, was a deceitful and joyless kind of planet.

Well then, was my grey humour just because I was under the need of shaking hands with Imre von N..., and saying, "A viszontlátásra!" ("Auf Wiedersehen!") or, more sensibly, saying to him "Goodbye?" Was that the real weight in my breast? I, a man—strong-willed, firm of temper and character! Surely I had other friends, many and warm ones, old ones, in a long row of places between Constantinople and London; in France, Germany, Austria, England. O dear, yes!... there were A.., and

B..., and C... and so, on very decently through a whole alphabet of amities. Why should I feel so fierce a hatred at this interrupting of a casual, pleasant but not extraordinary intimacy, quite one de voyage on its face, between two men, who, no matter how companionable, were of absolutely diverse races, unlike objects in life and wide-removed environments?... who could not even understand each other's mother-tongues? Why did existence itself seem so ironical, so full of false notes, so capricious in its kindness... seem allowed us that we might not be glad in it as... Elsewhere? The reply to each of these queries was close to another answer to another question; that one which Imre von N... had asked,.. "And why, pray, have you found yourself so wonderfully happy lately?" That I should find myself so wonderfully unhappy now? Perhaps so.

Imre was at the tram, and in high spirits.

"We shall have a beautiful afternoon, my dear fellow.... Beautiful!" he began. Then... "What the mischief is the matter with you? You look as if you had lost your soul!"

In a few words, I told him of my summons North.

"Nonsense!" he exclaimed. "You are making a bad joke!"

"Unfortunately I never have been less able to joke in my life! Tomorrow afternoon I must be off, as surely as Saint-Stephen's Crown has the Crooked Cross."

Imre "looked right, looked left, looked straight before". For an instant his look was almost painfully serious. Then it changed to an amused bewilderment. "Well... sudden things come by twos! You have got to start off for God knows where, tomorrow afternoon: I have got to be up at dawn, to rush my legs off! For, about noon I go out by a pokey special-train, to the Summer-Camp at P... And I must stay there five, six, ten mortal days, drilling Slovaks, and other such cattle! No wonder we have had a fine time of it here together! Too beautiful to last! But, Lord, how I envy you! Won't you change places with me? You're such an obliging fellow, Oswald! You go to the Camp: let me go to London?"

At this moment, up came the tram. It was packed with an excursion-party. We were hustled and separated during our leisurely transit. Imre met some fair acquaintances, and made himself exceedingly lively company to them, till we reached the Z... cross-road. We stepped out alone.

I did not break the silence as the noisy tram vanished, and the country's quietness closed us in.

"Well?" said Imre, after fully five minutes, as we approached the Z.... gateway.

"Well," I replied quite as laconically.

"Oh come, come," he began, "even if it is I routing out of bed by sunrise tomorrow, to start in for all that P.. Camp drudgery, and you to go spinning along in the afternoon to England... why, what of it! We mustn't let the tragedy spoil our last afternoon. Eh?... Philosophy, philosophy, my dear Oswald! I have grown so trained, as a soldier, to having every sort of personal plan and pleasure, great or small, simply blown to the winds on half-an-hour's notice, that I have ceased to get into bad humour over any such contretemps. What profits it? Life isn't at all a plaything for a good lot of us, more's the pity! We've got to suffer and be strong; or else learn not to suffer. That on the whole is decidedly preferable. Permit me to recommend it; a superior article for the trade, patent applied for, take only the genuine."

I was not in tune for being philosophic, in that moment. And, from the very first words and demeanour with which Imre had received the announcement that so cruelly preyed on my spirits, I was... shall I write piqued—by what seemed to be his indifference; nay more, by his complete nonchalance. Whether Imre as a soldier, or through possessing a colder nature than I had inferred.... at least, colder than some other natures... had indeed learned to sustain life's disagreeable surprises with equanimity, was nothing now to me. Or, stay, it was a good deal that just then came crosswise to my mood; so wholly intransigéant. Angry irritation waxed hot in me all at once, along with increasing bitterness of heart. It is edifying to observe what successive and sheer stupidities a man will perpetrate under such circumstances... edifying and pitiable!

"I don't at all envy you your philosophy, my dear friend," I said sharply. "I believe a good deal in the old notion as to philosophic people being pretty often unfeeling people... much too often. I think I'd rather not become a stoic. Stoic means a stock. I'm not so far along as you."

"Really? Oh, you try it and you'll like it... as the cannibals said to the priest who had to watch them eat up the bishop. It is far better to feel nothing than to feel unpleasant things too much... so much more comfortable and cheap in the end.... Ei! you over there!" he called out to a brown-skinned czigány lad, suddenly appearing out of a coppice, with something suspiciously like a snap-shot in his hand, "don't you let the házmester up at the house catch you with that thing about you, or you'll get yourself into trouble! Young poacher!" he added angrily... "those snap-shots when a gipsey handles them are as bad as a fowling-piece. The devil take the little rascal! And the devil take everything else!"

We walked down an alley in silence. Neither of us had ever been in this sort of a mood till this afternoon. The atmosphere was a trifle electric! Imre drew his sword and began giving slashes at trees and weeds, an undesirable habit that he had, as we strolled onward. Thought I, "A pleasing couple of hours truly we are likely to pass!" I felt that I would better have stayed at home; to start my packing-up for London. Then I pulled myself together. I found myself all at once possessed of a decent stock of pride, if not "philosophy". I undertook to meet Imre's manner, if not to match his sentiments. I began to talk suavely of trifles, then of more serious topics... of wholly general interests. I smiled much and laughed a little. I referred to my leaving Szent-Istvánhely and him... more to the former necessity... in precisely the neatest measure of tranquility and even of humour. Imre's responsiveness to this delicate return for his own indifference at once showed me that I had taken the right course not to "spoil this last afternoon together".... probably the last such in our lives!....

On one topic, most personal to Imre, I could speak with him at any time without danger of its being talk-worn between us; could argue with him about it even to forgetting any other matter in hand; if, alas! Imre was ever satirical, or placidly unresponsive toward it. That topic was his temperamental, obstinate indifference to making the most of himself in his profession; to "going-on" in it, with all natural energies or assumed ones. He was, as I have mentioned, a perfectly satisfactory officer. But there it ended. He seemed to think that he had done his duty, and must await such vague event as would carry him, motu proprio, further toward efficiency and distinction. Or else, of all things foolish, not to say discreditable, he declared he still would "keep his eyes open for a chance to enter civil life"... would give himself up to some more or less aesthetic calling, especially of a musical connection... become "free from this farce of playing soldier." He excused his plan by saying that his position now was "disgracefully insincere." Insincere, yes; but not disgraceful; and he was resting on his oars with the idea that he ought not to try to row on, just when such conduct was fatal. A man can remedy a good deal that he feels is an "insincere" attitude toward daily life. And what is more, any worthy, any elevating profession, and in the case of the soldier the sense of himself as a prop and moral element in the State must not be insulted! The army-life even if chosen merely from duty, and led in times of peace, is a good deal like the marriage of respect. The man may never have loved the wife to whom he is bound, he may never be able to love her, he may find her presence lamentably unsympathisch. But mere self-respect and the outward duty to her, and duty to those who are concerned in her honour as in his, in her welfare as in his.... there comes in the unavoidable and just demand! Honour and country are eloquent for a soldier, always. It was on the indispensable, unwelcome, ever-postponed Hadiskolai course that, once more, this afternoon, I found myself voluble with Imre. If I could not well speak of myself, I could of him, in a parting appeal.

"You must go on! You have no right to falter now. For God's sake, N.....! put by all these miserable dreams of quitting the service. What in the world could you do out of it? You have plenty of time for entertaining yourself with strumming and singing, and what not. Everything is in your own hands. Oh, yes, I know perfectly well that special help is needed to push one along fast... friends at court. But you are not wholly without them. For your father's sake and yours!.... You have shown already what you can do! If you will only work a bit harder! The War-School, Imre, the War-School! That must come. If you care for your own credit, success... stop, I forbid you to sneer... get into the School, hate it as much as you will!"

"I hate it! I hate it all, I tell you! I am sick of pretending to like it. Especially just lately... more so than ever!"

"Very possibly. But what of that? Is there anything else in the wide world that you feel you can do any better?... beginning such an experiment at twenty-five years of age.... with no training for so much as digging a ditch? Do you wish to become a dance-music strummer in the Városliget? Or a second-class acrobat in the Circus Wulff? Or will you throw off your uniform, to take flight to America... Australia... to be a riding-master or a waiter in a restaurant, or a vagabond, like some of the Habsburg arch-dukes? Imre, Imre! Instead be... a man! A man in this, as in all else. You trifle with your certainty of a career. Be a man in this matter!"

He sighed. Then softly, with a strange despair of life in his tone:

"Be a man? In this, as in all? God! how I wish I could be so."

"Wish you could be so! I don't know what you mean. A manlier fellow one need not be! Only this damnable neglect of your career! You surely wish to succeed in life?"

"I wish. But I cannot will..... Do not talk any more about it just now. You can... teremtette! you will write me quite enough about it. You are exactly like Karvaly, once that topic comes into your mind! Yes, like him to half-a-word... and I certainly am no match for either of you."

"I should think," returned I, coldly, "that if you possess any earnest, definite regard for such a zealous friend as Herr Karvaly, or for any true friend, you would prove it by just this very effort to make the most of yourself... for their sakes if not for your own."

I waited a second or so, as we stood there looking across an opening of the woodland. Then I added,— "For his sake, if not for—for such a newcomer's sake as—mine. But I begin to believe that your heart does not so easily stir really, warmly, as... as I supposed. At least, not for me. Possibly for nobody, my dear N...! Odd—for you have so many friends. I confess I don't see now just why. You are a strange fellow, Imre. Such a row of contradictions!"

One, two... one, two... again was Imre walking along in silence, exactly as on the evening when we came over the long Suspension Bridge in town together. And once more was he whistling softly, as if either wholly careless or buried in thought, those same two or three melancholy notes of what I had discovered was a little Bakony peasant-song, "O, jaj! az álom nelkül"—! ("Alas, I am sleepless,—I fear to dream!")

So passed more than an hour. We spoke less and less. My moods of self-forgetfulness, of philosophy, passed with it. I could not recover either.

We had made a detour around the lonelier portion of the park. The sun was fairly setting as we came out before the open lawn, wide, and uncropped save by two cows and a couple of farm-horses. There were trees on either border. At farther range, was the long, low mansion, three stories high, with countless white-painted croisées, and lime-blanched chimneys; an odd Austro-Magyar-style dwelling, of a long-past fashion, standing up solid and sharp against that silver-saffron sky. Not a sign of life, save those slow-moving beasts, far off in the middle of the lawn. No smoke from the yet more removed old homestead. Not a sound, except a gentle wind... melancholy and fitful. We two might have been remote, near a village in the Siebenbürgen; not within twenty minutes of a great commercial city.

Instead of going on toward the avenue which led to the exit—the hour being yet early—we sat down on a stone bench, much beaten by weather. A few steps away, rose the monument I have mentioned... "To the Unforgettable Memory" of Lorand and Egon Z...

Neither Imre nor I spoke immediately; each of us was a trifle leg-weary, I once more was sad and... angry. As we sat there, I read over for yet another time... the last time?... those carved words which reminded a reader, whether to his gladness of soul or dolour, that love, a love indeed strong as death, between two manly souls was no mere ideal; but instead, a possible crown of existence, a glory of life, a realizable unity that certain fortunate sons of men attained! A jewel that others must yearn for, in disappointment and folly, and with the taste of aloes, and the white of the egg, for the pomegranate and the honeycomb! I sighed.

"Oh, courage, courage, my well beloved friend!" exclaimed Imre, hearing the sigh and apparently quite misreading my innermost thoughts. "Don't be downhearted again as to leaving Szent-Istvánhely tomorrow; not to speak of being cheerful even if you must part from your most obedient servant. Such is life!... unless we are born sultans and kaisers... and if we are that, we must die to slow music in the course of time."

I vouchsafed no comment. Could this be Imre von N...? Certainly I had made the acquaintance of a new and extremely uncongenial Imre; in exactly the least appropriate circumstances to lose sight of the sympathetic, gentler-natured friend, whom I had begun to consider as one well understood, and had found responsive to a word, a look. Did all his closer friends meet, sooner or later, with this under-half of his temperament—this brusqueness which I had hitherto seen in his bearing with only his outside associates? Did they admire it... if caring for him? Bitterness came over me in a wave, it rose to my lips in a burst.

"It is just as well that one of us should show some feeling.... a trifle... when our parting is so near."

A pause. Then Imre:

"The 'one of us', that is to say the only one, who has any 'feeling' being yourself, my dear Oswald?"

"Apparently."

"Don't you think that perhaps you rather take things for granted? Or that, perhaps, you feel too much? That is, in supposing that I feel too little?"

My reply was quick and acid enough:

"Have you any sentiments in the matter worth calling by such a name, at all? I've not remarked them so far! Are friends that love you and value you only worth their day with you?... have they no real, lasting individuality for you? Your heart is not so difficult to please as mine; nor so difficult to occupy."

Again a brief interval. Imre was beating a tattoo on his braided cap, and examining the top of that article with much attention. The sky was less light now. The long, melancholy house had grown pallid against the foliage. Still the same fitful breeze. One of the cows lowed.

He looked up. He began speaking gravely... kindly.. not so much as if seeking his words for their exactness, but rather as if he were fearful of committing himself outwardly to some innermost process of thought. Afraid, more than unwilling.

"Listen, my dear friend. We must not expect too much of one another in this world... must we? Do not be foolish. You know well that one of the last things that I regard as 'of a day' is our friendship.. however suddenly grown. No matter what you think now... for just these few moments... when something disturbs us both... that you know. Why, dear friend! did I not believe it myself; had I not so soon after our meeting believed it..... do you think I would have shown you so much of my real self, happy or unhappy, for better or worse? Sides of my nature unknown to others. Traits that you like, along with traits that I see you do not like? Why Oswald, you understand me... the real me!—better than anybody else that I have ever met. Because I wished it... I hoped it. Because I—I could not help it. Just that. But you see the trouble is that, in spite of all... you do not wholly understand me. And... and the worst of the reason is that I am the one most to blame for it! And I... I cannot better it now."

"When do we understand one another in this life of half-truths... half-intimacies?"

"Yes... all too-often half... whether it is with one's wife, one's mistress, one's friend! And I am not easy... ah, how I have had to learn the way to keep myself so—to study it till it is a second nature to me!—I am not easy to know! But, Oswald, Oswald, ich kann nicht anders, nein, nein, ich kann nicht anders!"

And then, in his own language, dull and doggedly he added to himself— "Mit használ, mit használ az én nekem?"—(What matters it to me?)

He took my hand now, that was lying on the settle beside his own, and held it while he spoke; unconsciously clasping it tighter and tighter till it was in pain, or would have been so, had it not been, like his own, cold from sheer nervousness. He continued:

"One thing more. You seem to forget sometimes that I am a man, and that you too are a man. Not either of us a—woman. Forgive me—I speak frankly. We are both of us, you and I, a bit over-sensitive... exalté... in type. Isn't that so? You often suggest a... a... regard... so... what shall I call it?... so romantic,... heroic... passionate—a love indeed (and here his voice was suddenly broken)—something that I cannot accept from anybody without warning him back.. back! I mean back coming to me from any other man. Sometimes you have troubled me... frightened me. I cannot,—will not, try to tell you why this is so. But so it is. Our friendship must be friendship as the world of today accepts friendship! Yes—as the world of our day does. God! What else could it be to-day.. friendship? What else—to-day?"

"Not the friendship which is love, the love which is friendship?" I said in a low voice; indeed, as I now remember more than half to myself.

Imre was looking at the darkened sky, the grey lawn—into the vague distance... at whatsoever was visible save myself. Then his glance was caught by the ghostly marble of the monument to the young Z.... heroes, at which I too was staring. A tone of appeal came as he continued:

"Once more, I beg, I implore you, not to make the mistake of—of—thinking me cold-natured. I, cold-natured?.. Ah, ah! If you knew me better, you'd not pack that notion into your trunks for London! Instead, believe that I value unspeakably all your friendship for me, dear Oswald. Time will prove that. I have had no friend like you, I believe. But though friendship can be a passion... can cast a spell over us that we cannot comprehend nor unbind"... here he withdrew his hand and pointed to the memorial-stone set up for those two human hearts that after so ardently beating for each other, were now but dust... "it must be only a spiritual, manlike regard! The world thought otherwise once. The world thinks—as it thinks—now. And the world, our to-day's world, must decide for us all! Friendship now—now—must stay as the man of our day understands it, Oswald. That is, if the man deserves the name, and is not to be classed as some sort of an incomprehensible... womanish... outcast... counterfeit.... a miserable puzzle—born to be every genuine man's contempt!"

We had come, once more, suddenly, fully, and because of me, on the topic which we had touched on, that night of our Lánczhid walk! But this time I faced it, in a sense of fatality and finality; in a rash, desperate desire to tear a secret out of myself, to breathe free, to be true to myself, to speak out the past and the present, so strangely united in these last few weeks, to reserve nothing, cost what it might! My hour had come!

"You have asked me to listen to you!" I cried. Even now I feel the despair, I think I hear the accent of it, with which I spoke. "I have heard you! Now I want you to listen to me! I wish to tell you a story. It is out of one man's deepest yet daily life... my own life. Most of what I wish to tell happened long before I knew you. It was far away, it was in what used to be my own country. After I tell it, you will be one of very few people in all the world who have known... even suspected... what happened to me. In telling you, I trust you with my social honour... with all that is outwardly and inwardly myself. And I shall probably pay a penalty... just because you hear the wretched history, Imre... you! For, before it ends, it has to do with you; as well as with something that you have just spoken of—so fiercely! I mean—how far a man, deserving to be called a man, refusing, as surely as God lives and has made him, to believe that he is.... what did you call him?... 'a miserable, womanish, counterfeit... outcast'... even if he be incomprehensible to himself... how such a being can suffer and be ruined in his innermost life and peace, by a soul-tragedy which he nevertheless can hide—must hide! I could have told you all on the night that we talked, as we crossed the Lánczhid. No, that is not true! I could not then. But I can now. For I may never see you again. You talk of our 'knowing each other'! I wish you to know me. And I could never write you this, never! Will you hear me, Imre?—patiently?"

"I will hear you patiently—yes, Oswald—if you think it best to tell me. Of that pray think, carefully."

"It is best! I am tired of thinking of it. It is time you knew."

"And I am really concerned in it?"

"You are immediately concerned. That is to say, before it ends. You will see how."

"Then you would better go on... of course."

He consented thus, in the constrained but decided tone which I have indicated as so often recurring during the evening, adding— "I am ready, Oswald."

"From the time when I was a lad, Imre... a little child... I felt myself unlike other boys in one element of my nature. That one matter was my special sense, my passion, for the beauty, the dignity, the charm... the... what shall I say?... the loveableness of my own sex. I hid it, at least so far as, little by little, I came to realize its force. For, I soon perceived that most other lads had no such passionate sentiment, in any important measure of their natures, even when they were fine-strung, impressionable youths. There was nothing unmanly about me; nothing really unlike the rest of my friends in school, or in town-life. Though I was not a strong-built, or rough-spirited lad, I had plenty of pluck and muscle, and was as lively on the playground, and fully as indefatigable, as my chums. I had a good many friends; close ones, who liked me well. But I felt sure, more and more, from one year to another even of that boyhood time, that no lad of them all ever could or would care for me as much as I could and did care for one or another of them! Two or three episodes made that clear to me. These incidents made me, too, shyer and shyer of showing how my whole young nature, soul and body together, Imre—could be stirred with a veritable adoration for some boy-friend that I elected.. an adoration with a physical yearning in it—how intense was the appeal of bodily beauty, in a lad, or in a man of mature years."

"And yet, with that beauty, I looked for manliness, poise, will-power, dignity and strength in him. For, somehow I demanded those traits, always and clearly, whatever else I sought along with them. I say 'sought'; I can say, too, won—won often to nearness. But this other, more romantic, emotion in me... so strongly physical, sexual, as well as spiritual... it met with a really like and equal and full response once only. Just as my school-life was closing, with my sixteenth year (nearly my seventeenth) came a friendship with a newcomer into my classes, a lad of a year older than myself, of striking beauty of physique, and uncommon strength of character. This early relation embodied the same precocious, absolutely vehement passion (I can call it nothing else) on both sides. I had found my ideal! I had realized for the first time, completely, a type; a type which had haunted me from first consciousness of my mortal existence, Imre; one that is to haunt me till my last moment of it. All my immature but intensely ardent regard was returned. And then, after a few months together, my schoolmate, all at once, became ill during an epidemic in the town, was taken to his home, and died. I never saw him after he left me."

"It was my first great misery, Imre. It was literally unspeakable! For, I could not tell to anyone, I did not know how to explain even to myself, the manner in which my nature had gone out to my young mate, nor how his being spontaneously so had blent itself with mine. I was not seventeen years old, as I said. But I knew clearly now what it was to love thus, so as to forget oneself in another's life and death! But also I knew better than to talk of such things. So I never spoke of my dead mate."

"I grew older, I entered my professional studies, and I was very diligent with them. I lived in a great capital, I moved much in general society. I had a large and lively group of friends. But always, over and over, I realized that, in the kernel, at the very root and fibre of myself, there was the throb and glow, the ebb and the surge, the seeking as in a vain dream to realize again that passion of friendship which could so far transcend the cold modern idea of the tie; the Over-Friendship, the Love-Friendship of Hellas—which meant that between man and man could exist—the sexual-psychic love. That was still possible! I knew that now! I had read it in the verses or the prose of the

Greek and Latin and Oriental authours who have written out every shade of its beauty or unloveliness, its worth or debasements—from Theokritos to Martial, or Abu-Nuwas, to Platen, Michel Angelo, Shakespeare. I had learned it from the statues of sculptors, with those lines so often vivid with a merely physical male beauty—works which beget, which sprang from, the sense of it in a race. I had half-divined it in the music of a Beethoven and a Tschaikowsky before knowing facts in the life-stories of either of them—or of an hundred other tone-autobiographists."

"And I had recognized what it all meant to most people today!—from the disgust, scorn and laughter of my fellow-men when such an emotion was hinted at! I understood perfectly that a man must wear the Mask, if he, poor wretch! could neither abide at the bound of ordinary warmth of feeling for some friend of friends, that drew on his innermost nature; or if he were not content because the other stayed within that bound. Love between two men, however absorbing, however passionate, must not be—so one was assured—solemnly or in disgusted incredulity—a sexual love, a physical impulse and bond. That was now as ever, a nameless horror—a thing against all civilization, sanity, sex, Nature, God! Therefore, I was, of course... what then was I? Oh, I perceived it! I was that anachronism from old—that incomprehensible incident in God's human creation... the man-loving man! The man-loving man! whose whole heart can be given only to another man, and who when his spirit is passing into his beloved friend's keeping would demand, would surrender, the body with it. The man-loving man! He who seeks not merely a spiritual unity with him whom he loves, but seeks the embrace that joins two male human beings in a fusion that no woman's arms, no woman's kisses can ever realize. No woman's embrace? No, no!... for instead of that, either he cares not a whit for it, is indifferent to it, is smilingly scornful of it: or else he tolerates it, even in the wife he has married (not to speak of any less honourable ties) as an artifice, a mere quietus to that undeceived sexual passion burning in his nature; wasting his really unmated individuality, years-long. Or else he surrenders himself to some woman who bears his name, loves him—to her who perhaps in innocence and ignorance believes that she dominates every instinct of his sex!—making her a wife that she may bear to him children; or thinking that marriage may screen him, or even (vain hope) 'cure' him! But oftenest, he flies from any woman, as her sexual self; wholly shrinks from her as from nothing else created; avoids the very touch of a woman's hand in his own, any physical contact with woman, save in a calm cordiality, in a sexless and fraternal reserve, a passionless if yet warm... friendship! Not seldom he shudders (he may not know why) in something akin to dread and to loathing, though he may succeed in hiding it from wife or mistress, at any near approach of his strong male body to a woman's trivial, weak, feminine one, however fair, however harmonious in lines! Yes, even were she Aphrodite herself!"

"And yet, Imre, thousands, thousands, hundreds of thousands, of such human creatures as I am, have not in body, in mind, nor in all the sum of our virility, in all the detail of our outward selves, any openly womanish trait! Not one! It is only the ignoramus and the vulgar who nowadays think or talk of the homosexual as if he were an—hermaphrodite! In every feature and line and sinew and muscle, in every movement and accent and capability, we walk the world's ways as men. We hew our ways through it as men, with vigour, success, honour... one master-instinct unsuspected by society for, it may be, our lives long! We plough the globe's roughest seas as men, we rule its States as men, we direct its finance and commerce as men, we forge its steel as men, we grapple with all its sciences, we triumph in all its arts as men, we fill its gravest professions as men, we fight in the bravest ranks of its armies as men, or we plan out its fiercest and most triumphant battles as men.... in all this, in so much more, we are men! Why, (in a bitter paradox) one can say that we always have been, we always are, always will be, too much men! So super-male, so utterly unreceptive of what is not manly, so aloof from any feminine essences, that we cannot tolerate woman at all as a sexual factor! Are we not the extreme of the male? its supreme phase, its outermost phalanx?—its climax of the aristocratic, the All-Man? And yet, if love is to be only what the narrow, modern, Jewish-Christian ethics of today declare it, if what they insist be the only natural and pure expression of 'the will to possess, the wish to surrender'.. oh, then is the flouting world quite right! For then we are indeed not men! But if not so, what are we? Answer that, who can!"

"The more perplexed I became in all this wretchedness (for it had grown to that by the time I had reached my majority).. the more perplexed I became because so often in books, old ones or new, nay, in the very chronicles of the criminal-courts, I came face to face with the fact that though tens of thousands of men, in all epochs, of noblest natures, of most brilliant minds and gifts, of intensest energies.. scores of pure spirits, deep philosophers, bravest soldiers, highest poets and artists, had been such as myself in this mystic sex-disorganization.... that nevertheless of this same Race, the Race-Homosexual, had been also, and apparently ever would be, countless ignoble, trivial, loathesome, feeble-souled and feeble-bodied creatures!... the very weaklings and rubbish of humanity!"

"Those, those, terrified me, Imre! To think of them shamed me; those types of man-loving-men who, by thousands, live incapable of any noble ideals or lives. Ah, those patently depraved, noxious, flaccid, gross, womanish beings! perverted and imperfect in moral nature and in even their bodily tissues! Those homosexual legions that are the straw-chaff of society; good for nothing except the fire that purges the world of garbage and rubbish! A Heliogabalus, a Gilles de Rais, a Henri Trois, a Marquis de Sade; the painted male-prostitutes of the boulevards and twilight-glooming squares! The effeminate artists, the sugary and fibreless musicians! The Lady Nancyish, rich young men of higher or lower society; twaddling aesthetic sophistries; stinking with perfume like cocottes! The second-rate poets and the neurasthenic, précieux poetasters who rhyme forth their forged literary passports out of their mere human decadence; out of their marrowless shams of all that is a man's fancy, a man's heart, a man's love-life! The cynical debauchers of little boys; the pederastic perverters of clean-minded lads in their teens; the white-haired satyrs of clubs and latrines!"

"What a contrast are these to great Oriental princes and to the heroes and heroic intellects of Greece and Rome! To a Themistocles, an Agesilaus, an Aristides and a Kleomenes; to Socrates and Plato, and Saint Augustine, to Servetus and Beza; to Alexander, Julius Caesar, Augustus, and Hadrian; to Prince Eugene of Savoy, to Sweden's Charles the Twelfth, to Frederic the Great, to indomitable Tilly, to the fiery Skobeleff, the austere Gordon, the ill-starred Macdonald; to the brightest lyrists and dramatists of old Hellas and Italia; to Shakespeare, (to Marlowe also, we can well believe) Platen, Grillparzer, Hölderlin, Byron, Whitman; to an Isaac Newton, a Justus Liebig—to Michel-Angelo and Sodoma; to the masterly Jerome Duquesnoy, the classic-souled Winckelmann, to Mirabeau, Beethoven, Bavaria's unhappy King Ludwig;—to an endless procession of exceptional men, from epoch to epoch! Yet as to these and innumerable others, facts of their hidden, inner lives have proved without shadow of doubt (however rigidly suppressed as 'popular information') or inferences vivid enough to silence scornful denial, have pointed out that they belonged to Us."

"Nevertheless, did not the widest overlook of the record of Uranianism, the average facts about one, suggest that the most part of homosexual humanity had always belonged, always would belong, to the worthless or the wicked? Was our Race gold or excrement!—as rubies or as carrion? If that last were one's final idea, why then all those other men, the Normalists, aye, our severest judges, those others whether good or bad, whether vessels of honour or dishonour, who are not in their love-instincts as are we... the millions against our tens of thousands, even if some of us are to be respected.... why, they do right to cast us out of society; for, after all, we must be just a vitiated breed!... We must be judged by our commoner mass.

"And yet, the rest of us! The Rest, over and over! men so high-minded, often of such deserved honour from all that world which has either known nothing of their sexual lives, or else has perceived vaguely, and with a tacit, a reluctant pardon! Could one really believe in God as making man to live at all, and to love at all, and yet at the same time believe that this love is not created, too, by God? is not of God's own divinest Nature, rightfully, eternally—in millions of hearts?... Could one believe that the eternal human essence is in its texture today so different from itself of immemorial time before now, whether Greek, Latin, Persian, or English? Could one somehow find in his spirit no dread through this, none, at the idea of facing God, as his Judge, at any instant?... could one feel at moments such strength of confidence that what was in him so was righteousness... oh, could all this be?—and yet must a man shudder before himself as a monster, a solitary and pernicious being—diseased, leprous, gangrened—one that must stagger along on the road of life, ever justly shunned, ever justly bleeding and ever the more wearied, till Death would meet him and say 'Come—enough!—Be free of all!—be free of thyself most of all!'"

I paused. Doing so, I heard from Imre, who had not spoken so much as a word—was it a sigh? Or a broken murmur of something coming to his lips in his own tongue? Was it—no, impossible!... was it a sort of sob, strangled in his throat? The evening had grown so dark that I could not have seen his face, even had I wished to look into it. However... absorbed now in my own tenebrous retrospect, almost forgetting that anyone was there, at my side, I went on:

"You must not think that I had not had friendships of much depth, Imre, which were not, first and last, quite free from this other accent in them. Yes, I had had such; and I have many such now; comradeships with men younger, men of my own age, men older, for whom I feel warm affection and admiration, whose company was and is a true happiness for me. But somehow they were not and, no matter what they are they still are not, of the Type; of that eternal, mysteriously-disturbing cruel Type, which so vibrates sexually against my hidden Self."

"How I dreaded, yet sought that Type!... how soon was I relieved, or dull of heart, when I knew that this or that friend was not enough dear to me, however dear he was, to give me that hated sexual stir and sympathy, that inner, involuntary thrill! Yet I sought it ever, right and left, since none embodied it for me;

while I always feared that some one might embody it! There were approaches to it. Then, then, I suffered or throbbed with a wordless pain or joy of life, at one and the same time! But fortunately these encounters failed of full realization. Or what might have been my fate passed me by on the other side. But I learned from them how I could feel toward the man who could be in his mind and body my ideal; my supremest Friend. Would I ever meet him?... meet him again?... I could say to myself— remembering that episode of my schooldays. Or would I never meet him! God forbid that! For to be all my life alone, year after year, striving to content myself with pleasant shadow instead of glowing verity!... Ah, I could well exclaim in the cry of Platen:

O, weh Dir, der die Welt verachtet, allein zu sein
Und dessen ganze Seele schmachtet allein zu sein!

"One day a book came to my hand. It was a serious work, on abnormalisms in mankind: a book partly psychologic, partly medico-psychiatric; of the newest 'school'. It had much to say of homosexualism, of Uranianism. It considered and discussed especially researches by German physicians into it. It described myself, my secret, unrestful self, with an unsparing exactness! The writer was a famous specialistic physician in nervous diseases, abnormal conditions of the mind, and so on—an American. For the first time I understood that responsible physicians, great psychologists—profound students of humanities, high jurists, other men in the world besides obscene humourists of a club-room, and judges and juries in police-courts—knew of men like myself and took them as serious problems for study, far from wholly despicable. This doctor spoke of my kind as simply—diseased. 'Curable', absolutely 'curable'; so long as the mind was manlike in all else, the body firm and normal. Certainly that was my case! Would I not therefore do well to take one step which was stated to be most wise and helpful toward correcting as perturbed a relation as mine had become to ordinary life? That step was—to marry. To marry immediately!"

"The physician who had written that book happened to be in England at the time. I had never thought it possible that I could feel courage to go to any man... save that one vague sympathizer, my dream-friend, he who some day would understand all!.. and confess myself; lay bare my mysterious nature. But if it were a mere disease, oh, that made a difference! So I visited the distinguished specialist at once. He helped me urbanely through my embarrassing story of my... 'malady'.... 'Oh, there was nothing extraordinary, not at all extraordinary in it, from the beginning to the end,' the doctor assured me, smiling. In fact, it was 'exceedingly common... All confidential specialists in nervous diseases knew of hundreds of just such cases. Nay, of much worse ones, and treated and cured them... A morbid state of certain sexual-sensory nerve-centers'... and so on, in his glib professional diagnosis."

"So I am to understand that I am curable?"— "Curable? Why, surely. Exactly as I have written in my work; as Doctor So-and-So, and the great psychiatric Professor Such-a-One, proved long ago... Your case my dear sir, is the easier because you suffer in a sentimental and sexual way from what we call the obsession of a set, distinct Type, you see; instead of a general... h'm... how shall I style it... morbidity of your inclinations. It is largely mere imagination! You say you have never really "realized" this haunting masculine Type which has given you such trouble? My dear sir, don't think any more about such nonsense!... you never will "realize" it in any way to be... h'm... disturbed. Probably had you married and settled down pleasantly, years ago, you often would have laughed heartily at the whole story of such an illusion of your nature now. Too much thought of it all, my dear friend! too much introspection, idealism, sedentary life, dear sir! Yes, yes, you must marry—God bless you!'"

"I paid my distinguished specialist his fee and came away, with a far lighter heart than I had had in many a year."

"Marry! Well, that was easily to be done. I was popular enough with women of all sorts. I was no woman-hater. I had many true and charming and most affectionate friendships with women. For, you must know, Imre, that such men as I am are often most attractive to women, most beloved by them.. I mean by good women... far more than through being their relatives and social friends. They do not understand the reason of our attraction for them, of their confidence, their strengthening sentiment. For we seldom betray to them our secret, and they seldom have knowledge, or instinct, to guess its mystery. But alas! it is the irony of our nature that we cannot return to any woman, except by a lie of the body and the spirit, (often being unable to compass or to endure that wretched subterfuge) a warmer glow than affection's calmest pulsations. Several times, before my consulting Dr. D... I had had the opportunity of marrying 'happily and wisely'—if marriage with any woman could have meant only a friendship. Naught physical, no responsibility of sex toward the wife to whom one gives oneself. But 'the will to possess, the desire to surrender', the negation of what is ourself which comes with the arms of some one other human creature about us—ours about him—long before, had I understood that the like of this joy was not possible for me with wife or mistress. It had seemed to me hopeless of attempt. If marriage exact that effort.. good God! then it means a growing wretchedness, riddle and mystery for two human beings, not for one. Stay! it means worse still, should they not be childless......"

"But now I had my prescription, and I was to be cured. In ten days, Imre, I was betrothed. Do not be surprised. I had known a long while earlier that I was loved. My betrothed was the daughter of a valued family friend, living in a near town. She was beautiful, gifted, young, high-souled and gentle. I had always admired her warmly; we had been much thrown together. I had avoided her lately however, because—unmistakeably—I had become sure of a deeper sentiment on her part than I could exchange."

"But now, now, I persuaded myself that I did indeed return it; that I had not understood myself. And confidently, even ardently, I played my new role so well, Imre, that I was deceived myself. And she? She never felt the shade of suspicion. I fancied that I loved her. Besides, my betrothed was not exacting, Imre. In fact, as I now think over those few weeks of our deeper intimacy, I can discern how I was favoured in my new relationship to her by her sensitive, maidenly shrinking from the physical nearness, even the touch, of the man who was dear to her... how troubling the sense of any man's advancing physical dominancy over her. Yet do not make the mistake of thinking that she was cold in her calm womanliness; or would have held herself aloof as a wife. It was simply virginal, instinctive reserve. She loved me; and she would have given herself wholly to me, as my bride."

"The date for our marriage was set. I tried to think of nothing but it and her; of how calmly, securely happy I should soon be, and of all the happiness that, God willing, I would bring into her young life. I say 'tried' to think of nothing else. I almost succeeded. But... nevertheless... in moments..."

"It was not to be, however, this deliverance, this salvation for me!"

"One evening, I was asked by a friend to come to his lodgings to dine, to meet some strangers, his guests. I went. Among the men who came was one... I had never seen him before... newly arrived in my city.. coming to pass the winter. From the instant that set me face to face with him... that let me hear his voice in only a greeting... that put us to exchanging a few commonplace sentences... I thrilled with joy and trembled to my innermost soul with a sudden anguish. For, Imre, it was as if that dead schoolmate of mine, not merely as death had taken him; but matured, a man in his beauty and charm... it was as if every acquaintance that ever had quickened within me the same unspeakable sense of a mysterious bond of soul and of body... the Man-Type which owned me and ever must own me, soul and body together—had started forth in a perfect avatar. Out of the slumberous past, out of the kingdom of illusions, straying to me from the realm of banished hopes, it had come to me! The Man, the Type, that thing which meant for me the fires of passion not to be quenched, that subjection of my whole being to an ideal of my own sex... that fatal 'nervous illusion', as the famous doctor's book so summarily ranged it for the world.. all had overtaken me again! My peace was gone—if ever I had had true peace. I was lost, with it!..."

"From that night, I forgot everything else except him. My former, unchanged, unchangeable self, in all its misery and mystery reverted. The temperament which I had thought to put to sleep, the invisible nature I had believed I could strangle—it had awakened with the lava-seethe of a volcano. It burned in my spirit and body, like a masked crater."

"Imre, I sought the friendship of this man, of my ideal who had re-created for me, simply by his existence, a world of feeling; one of suffering and yet of delight. And I won his friendship! Do not suppose that I dared to dream, then or ever, of more than a commonplace, social intimacy. Never, never! Merely to achieve his regard toward myself a little more than toward others; merely that he would care to give me more of his society, would show me more of his inner self than he inclined to open to others. Just to be accounted by him somewhat dearer, in such a man's vague often elusive degree, than the majority for whom he cared at all! Only to have more constant leave to delight my spirit in silence with his physical beauty while guarding from him in a sort of terror the psychic effects it wrought in me..... My hopes went no further than these. And, as I say, I won them. As it kindly happened, our tastes, our interests in arts and letters, our temperaments, the fact that he came to my city with few acquaintances in it and was not a man who readily seeks them... the chance that he lived almost in the same house with me... such circumstances favored me immediately. But I did not deceive myself once, either as to what was the measure or the kind of my emotion for him, any more than about what (if stretched to its uttermost) would be his sentiment for me, for any man. He could not love a man so. He could love... passionately, and to the completing of his sexual nature... only a woman. He was the normal, I the abnormal. In that, alone, he failed to meet all that was I:

"O, the little more, and how much it is!

And the little less.. and what worlds away!"

"Did I keep my secret perfectly from him? Perfectly, Imre! You will soon see that clearly. There were times when the storm came full over me… when I avoided him, when I would have fled from myself, in the fierce struggle. But I was vigilant. He was moved, now and then, at a certain inevitable tenderness that I would show him. He often spoke wonderingly of the degree of my 'absorbing friendship'. But he was a man of fine and romantic ideals, of a strong and warm temper. His life had been something solitary from his earliest youth… and he was no psychologist. Despite many a contest with our relationship, I never allowed myself to complain of him. I was too well aware how fortunate was my bond with him. The man esteemed me, trusted me, admired me… all this thoroughly. I had more; for I possessed what in such a nature as his proves itself a manly affection. I was an essential element in his daily life all that winter; intimate to a depth that (as he told me, and I believe it was wholly true) he had never expected another man could attain. Was all that not enough for me? Oh, yes! and yet… and yet…"

"I will not speak to you more of that time which came to pass for me, Imre. It was for me, verily, a new existence! It was much such a daily life, Imre, as you and I might lead together, had fate allowed us the time for it to ripen. Perhaps we yet might lead it… God knows!… I leave you tomorrow!"

"But, you ask,—what of my marriage-engagement?"

"I broke it. I had broken it within a week after I met him, so far as shattering, it to myself went. I knew that no marriage, of any kind yet tolerated in our era, would 'cure' me of my 'illusion', my 'nervous disease', could banish this 'mere psychic disturbance', the result of 'too much introspection.' I had no disease! No… I was simply what I was born!—a complete human being, of firm, perfect physical and mental health; outwardly in full key with all the man's world: but, in spite of that, a being who from birth was of a vague, special sex; a member of the sex within the most obvious sexes, or apart from them. I was created as a man perfectly male, save in the one thing which keeps such a 'man' back from possibility of ever becoming integrally male— his terrible, instinctive demand for a psychic and a physical union with a man—not with a woman."

"Presently, during that same winter, accident opened my eyes wider to myself. From then, I have needed no further knowledge from the Tree of my Good and Evil. I met with a mass of serious studies, German, Italian, French, English, from the chief European specialists and theorists on the similisexual topic: many of them with quite other views than those of my well-meaning but far too conclusive Yankee doctor. I learned of the much-discussed theories of 'secondary sexes' and 'intersexes'. I learned of the theories and facts of homosexualism, of the Uranian Love, of the Uranian Race, of 'the Sex within a Sex'. I could, at last, inform myself fully of its mystery, and of the logical, inevitable and necessary place in sexualism, of the similisexual man, and of the similisexual woman".

"I came to know their enormous distribution all over the world today; and of the grave attention that European scientists and jurists have been devoting to problems concerned with homosexualism. I could pursue intelligently the growing efforts to set right the public mind as to so ineradicable and misunderstood a phase of humanity. I realized that I had always been a member of that hidden brotherhood and Sub-Sex, or Super-Sex. In wonder, too I informed myself of its deep, instinctive, freemasonries—even to organized ones—in every social class, every land, every civilization: of the signs and symbols and safeguards of concealment. I could guess that my father, my grandfather and God knows how many earlier forerunners of my unhappy Ego, had been of it! 'Cure?' By marriage? By marriage, when my blood ran cold at the thought!...... The idea was madness, in a double sense. Better a pistol-shot to my heart! So first, I found pretexts to excuse meetings with my bride-not-to-be, avoiding thus a comedy which now was odious as a lie and insupportable as a nervous demand. Next, I pleaded business-worries. So the marriage was postponed for three months further. Then I discovered a new obstacle to bring forward. With that, the date of the wedding was made indefinite. Then came some idle gossip, unjust reflections on my betrothed and on myself. I knew well where blame enough should fall, but not that sort of blame. An end had to be! I wrote my betrothed, begging my freedom, giving no reason.

She released me, telling me that she would never marry any other man. She keeps her word to-day. I drew my breath in shame at my deliverance.

"Any other man!"

"So seldom had I referred to my betrothal in talking with my new friend that he asked me no questions when I told him it was ended. He mistook my reserve; and respected it rigidly."

"During that winter, I was able to prove myself a friend in deed and need to him. Twice, by strange fatality, a dark cloud came over his head. I might not dare to show him that he was dearer than myself; but I could protect and aid him. For, do not think that he had no faults. He had more than few; he was no hero, no Galahad. He was careless, he was foolishly obstinate, he made missteps; and punishment came. But not further than near. For I stood between! At another time his over-confidence in himself, his unsuspiciousness, almost brought him to ruin, with a shameful scandal! I saved him, stopping the mouths of the dogs that were ready to howl, as well as to tear. I did so at the cost of impairing my own material welfare; worse still, alas! with a question of duty to others. Then, once again, as that year passed, he became involved in a difference, in which certain of my own relatives, along with some near friends of my family were concerned; directors in a financial establishment in our city. I took his part. By that step, I sacrificed the good-will and the longtime intimacy of the others. What did I care? 'The world well lost!' thought I."

"Then, from that calm sky, thickened and fell on me the storm; and for my goodly vineyard I had Desolation!"

"One holiday, he happened to visit some friends in the town where was living my betrothed.. that had been. He heard there, in a club's smoking-room, a tale 'explaining'—positively and circumstantially, why my engagement had been broken. The story was a silly falsehood; but it reflected on my honour. He defended me instantly and warmly. That I heard. But his host, after the sharp passing altercation was over, the evening ended, took him aside to tell him privately that, while friendship for me made it a credit to stand out for me, the tale was 'absolutely true'.

He returned to me late that night. He was thoroughly annoyed and excited. He asked me, as I valued my good name and his public defence of it, to give him, then and there, the real, the decisive reason for my withdrawing from my engagement. He would not speak of it to anyone; but he would be glad to know, now, on what ground he rested. I admitted that my betrothed had not wished the withdrawing."

"That was the first thing counter to what he had insisted at the club. He frowned in perplexity. Ah, so the matter was wholly from myself? I assented. Would I further explain?... so that at least he could get rid of one certain local statement... of that other one. An argument rose between us that grew to a sharp altercation. It was our first one, as well as our last. We became thoroughly angry, I the more so, because of what I felt was a manifest injustice to myself. Finally there was no other thing left than for me to meet his appeal—his demand. 'No matter what was the root of the mystery, no matter what any attitude toward me because of it, he must know'... Still I hung back. Then, solemnly, he pledged me his word that whatever I might disclose, he 'would forgive it'; it should 'never be mentioned between us two again'; only provided that it bore out his defence of my relation to a faithful and pure woman."

"So—I yielded! Lately, the maddening wish to tell him all at any risks, the pressure of passion and its concealment... they had never so fiercely attacked me! In a kind of exalted shame, but in absolute sincerity, I told him all! I asked nothing from him, except his sympathy, his belief in whatever was my higher and manlier nature... as the world judges any man... and the toleration of our friendship on the lines of its past. Nothing more: not a handclasp, not a look, not a thought more; the mere continued sufferance of my regard. Never again need pass between us so much as a syllable or a glance to remind him of this pitiable confession from me, to betray again the mysterious fire that burned in me underneath our intimacy. He had not suspected anything of it before. It could be forgotten by him from now, onward."

"Did I ask too much? By the God that made mankind, Imre—

that made it not only male or female but also as We are... I do not think I did!"

"But he, he thought otherwise! He heard my confession through with ever more hostile eyes, with an astonished unsympathy... disgust... curling his lips. Then, he spoke— slowly—pitilessly: '... I have heard that such creatures as you describe yourself are to be found among mankind. I do not know, nor do I care to know, whether they are a sex by themselves, a justified, because helpless, play of Nature; or even a kind of logically essential link, a between-step.... as you seem to have persuaded yourself. Let all that be as it may be. I am not a man of science nor keen to such new notions! From this moment, you and I are strangers! I took you for my friend because I believed you to be a... man. You chose me for your friend because you believed me.... stay, I will not say that!... because you wished me to be.... a something else, a something more or less like to yourself, whatever you are! I loathe you!... I loathe you! When I think that I have touched your hand, have sat in the same room with you, have respected you!.. Farewell!...... If I served you as a man should serve such beings as you, this town should know your story tomorrow! Society needs more policemen than it has, to protect itself from such lepers as you! I will keep your hideous secret. Only remember never to speak to me!... never to look my way again! Never! From henceforward I have never known you and never will think of you!—if I can forget anything so monstrous in this world!'"

"So passed he out of my life, Imre. Forever! Over the rupture of our friendship not much was said, nevertheless. For he was called to London a few days after that last interview; and he was obliged to remain in the capital for months. Meantime I had changed my life to meet its new conditions; to avoid gossip. I had removed my lodgings to a suburb. I had taken up a new course in professional work. It needed all my time. Then, a few months later, I started quietly on a long travel-route on the Continent, under excuse of ill-health. I was far from being a stranger to life in at least half a dozen countries of Europe, east or west. But now, now, I knew that it was to be a refuge, an exile!"

"For so began those interminable, those mysterious, restless pilgrimages, with no set goals for me; those roamings alone, of which even the wider world, not to say this or that circle of friends, has spoken with curiosity and regret. My unexplained and perpetual exile from all that earlier meant home, sphere, career, life! My wandering and wandering, ever striving to forget, ever struggling to be beguiled intellectually at least; to be diverted from so profound a sense of loss. Or to attain a sort of emotional assoupissement, to feel myself identified with new scenes, to achieve a new identity. Little by little, my birth-land, my people, became strange to me. I grew wholly indifferent to them. I turned my back fuller on them, evermore. The social elements, the grades of humanity really mine, the concerns of letters, of arts,... from these I divorced myself utterly. They knew me no more. In some of them, already I had won a certain repute; but I threw away its culture as one casts aside some plant that does not seem to him worth watering and tending."

"And indeed the zest of these things, their reason for being mine, seemed dead.... asphyxiated! For, they had grown to be so much a part of what had been the very tissue of intimacy, of life, with him! I fled them all. Never now did my foot cross the threshold of a picture-gallery, never did I look twice at the placard of a theater, never would I enter a concert-room or an opera-house, never did I care to read a romance, a poem, or to speak with any living creature of aesthetics that had once so appealed to me! Above all did my aversion to music (for so many years a peculiar interest for me)—become now a dull hatred,..... a detestation, a contempt, a horror!... super-neurotic, quintessently sexual, perniciously homosexual art—mystery— that music is! For me, no more symphonies, no more sonatas, no more songs!... No more exultations, elegies, questions to Fate of any orchestra!... Nevermore!"

"And yet, involuntarily, sub-consciously, I was always hoping... seeking—something. Hoping..., seeking.... what? Another such man as I? Sometimes I cried out as to that, 'God forbid it!' For I dreaded such a chance now; realizing the more what it would most likely not offer me. And really unless a miracle of miracles were to be wrought just for me, unless I should light upon another human creature who in sympathies, idealisms, noble impulses, manliness and a virile life could fill, and could wish to fill, the desolate solitudes of mine, could confirm all that was deepest fixed in my soul as the concept of true similisexual masculinity.... oh, far better meet none! For such a miracle of miracles I should not hope. Even traversing all the devious ways of life may not bring us face to face with such a friend. Yet I was hoping—seeking—I say: even if there was no vigour of expectancy, but rather in my mind the melancholy lines of the poet:

> *And are there found two souls, that each the other*
> *Wholly shall understand? Long must man search*
> *In that deep riddle—seek that Other soul*
> *Until he dies! Seeking, despairing—dies!*

"Or, how easy to meet such a man, he also 'seeking, despairing' and not to recognize him, any more than he recognizes us! The Mask—the eternal social Mask for the homosexual!—worn before our nearest and dearest, or we are ruined and cast out! I resolved to be content with tranquility... pleasant friendships. Something like a kindly apathy, often possessed me."

"And nevertheless, the Type that still so stirred my nature? The man that is.... inevitably.. to be loved, not merely liked; to be feared while yet sought; the friend from whom I can expect nothing, from whom never again will I expect anything, more than calm regard, his sympathy, his mere leave for my calling him 'barátom'—my brother-friend? He, by whom I should at least be respected as an upright fellow-creature from the workshop of God, not from the hand of the Devil; be taken into companionship because of what in me is worthily companionable? The fellow-man who will accept what of good in me is like the rest of men, nor draw away from me, as from a leper? Have I really ceased to dream of this grace for me, this vision—as years have passed?"

"Never, alas! I have been haunted by it; however suppressed in my heart. And something like its embodiment has crossed my way, really nearly granted me again; more than once. There was a young English officer, with whom I was thrown for many weeks, in a remote Northern city. We became friends; and the confidence between us was so great that I trusted him with the knowledge of what I am. And therewith had I in turn, a confession from him of a like misfortune, the story of his passion for a brother-officer in a foreign service, that made him one of the most wretched men on the face of the world—while everyone in his circle of home-intimates and regimental friends fancied that he had not a trouble in life! There was, too, one summer in Bosnia, a meeting with a young Austrian architect; a fellow of noble beauty and of high, rich nature. There was a Polish friend, a physician—now far off in Galizien. There was an Italian painter in Rome. But such incidents were not full in the key. Hence, they moved me only so far and no farther. Other passings and meetings came. Warm friendship often grew out of them; tranquil, lasting, sustaining friendship!—that soul-bond not over-common with us, but, when really welded, so beautiful, so true, so enduring!..."

"But one thing I had sworn, Imre; and I have kept my word! That so surely as ever again I may find myself even half-way drawn to a man by the inner passion of an Uranian love—not by the mere friendship of a colder psychic complexion—if that man really shows me that he cares for me with respect, with intimate affection, with trust... then he shall know absolutely what manner of man I am! He shall be shown frankly with what deeper than common regard he has become a part of my soul and life! He shall be put to a test!... with no shrinkings on my part. Better break apart early, than later... if he say that we break! Never again, if unquiet with such a passion, would I attempt to wear to the end the mask, to fight out the lie, the struggle! I must be taken as I am, pardoned for what I am; or neither pardoned nor taken. I have learned my lesson once and well. But the need of my maintaining such painful honesty has come seldom. I have been growing in to expecting no more of life, no realizing whatever of the Type that had been my undoing, that must mean always my peace or my deepest unrest... till I met you, Imre! Till I met you!"

"Met you! Yes, and a strange matter in my immediately passionate interest in you... another one of the coincidences in our interest for each other... is the racial blood that runs in your veins. You are a Magyar. You have not now to be told of the unexplainable, the mysterious affinity between myself and your race and nation; of my sensitiveness, ever since I was a child, to the chord which Magyarország and the Magyar sound in my heart. Years have only added to it, till thy land, thy people, Imre, are they not almost my land, my people? Now I have met thee. Thou wert to be; somewhat, at least, to be for me! That thou wast ordained to come into the world that I should love thee, no matter what thy race... that I believe! But, see! Fate also has willed that thou shouldst be Magyar, one of the Children of Emesa, one of the Folk of Árpád!"

"I cannot tell thee, Imre,... oh, I have no need now to try!.... what thou hast become for me. My Search ended when thou and I met. Never has my dream given me what is this reality of thyself. I love this world now only because thou art in it. I respect thee wholly—I respect myself—certain, too, of that coming time, however far away now, when no man shall ever meet any intelligent civilization's disrespect simply because he is similisexual, Uranian! But—oh, Imre, Imre!—I love thee, as can love only the Uranian... once more helpless, and therewith hopeless!—but this time no longer silent, before the Friendship which is Love, the Love which is Friendship."

"Speak my sentence. I make no plea. I have kept my pledge to confess myself tonight. But I would have fulfilled it only a little later, were I not going away from thee tomorrow. I ask nothing, except what I asked long ago of that other, of whom I have told thee! Endure my memory, as thy friend! Friend? That at least! For, I would say farewell, believing that I shall still have the right to call thee 'friend'—even—O God!—when I remember tonight. But whether that right is to be mine, or not, is for thee to say. Tell me!"

I stopped.

Full darkness was now about us. Stillness had so deepened that the ceasing of my own low voice made it the more suspenseful. The sweep of the night-wind rose among the acacias. The birds of shadow flitted about us. The gloom seemed to have entered my soul—as Death into Life. Would Imre ever speak?

His voice came at last. Never had I heard it so moved, so melancholy. A profound tenderness was in every syllable.

"If I could... my God! if I only could!.. say to thee what I cannot. Perhaps... some time.... Forgive me, but thou breakest my heart!.... Not because I care less for thee as my friend.... no, above all else, not that reason! We stay together, Oswald!... We shall always be what we have become to each other! Oh, we cannot change, not through all our lives! Not in death, not in anything! Oh, Oswald! that thou couldst think, for an instant, that I—I—would dream of turning away from thee... suffer a break for us two... because thou art made in thy nature as God makes mankind—as each and all, or not as each and all! We are what we are!... This terrible life of ours... this existence that men insist on believing is almost all to be understood nowadays— probed through and through—decided!... but that ever was and will be just mystery, all!...... Friendship between us? Oh, whether we are near or far! Forever! Forever, Oswald!... Here, take my hand! As long as I live... and beyond then! Yes, by God above us, by God in us!... Only, only, for the sake of the bond between us from this night, promise me that thou wilt never speak again of what thou hast told me of thyself—never, unless I break the silence. Nevermore a word of—of thy—thy—feeling for me. There are other things for us to talk of, my dear brother? Thou wilt promise?"

With his hand in mine, my heart so lightened that I was as a new creature, forgetting even the separation before me, I promised. Gladly, too. For, instead of loss, with this parting, what gain was mine! Imre knew me now as myself!—he really knew me: and yet was now rather the more my friend than less, so I could believe, after this tale of mine had been told him! His sympathy—his respect—his confidence—his affection—his continued and deeper share in my strange and lonely life—even if lands and seas should divide us two—ah, in those instants of my reaction and relief, it seemed to me that I had everything that my heart had ever sought of him, or would seek! I made the promise too, gladly with all my soul. Why should he or I ever speak of any stranger emotions again?

Abruptly, after another long pressure of my hand, my friend started up.

"Oswald we must go home!" he exclaimed. "It's nearly nine o'clock, surely. I have a regimental report to look at before ten... this affair of mine tomorrow."

Nearly the whole of our return-ride we were silent. The tram was full as before with noisy pleasure-trippers. Even after quitting the vehicle, neither of us said more than a few sentences... the beauty of the night, the charm of the old Z... park, and so on. But again Imre kept his arm in mine, all the way we walked. It was, I knew, not accident. It was the slight sign of earnest thoughts, that he did not care to utter in so many words.

We came toward my hotel.

"I shall not say farewell tonight, Oswald," said Imre, "you know how I hate farewells at any time... hate them as much as you. There is more than enough of such a business. Much better to be sensible.. to add as few as one can to the list.... I will look in on you tomorrow... about ten o'clock. I don't start till past midday."

I assented. I was no longer disturbed by any mortal concerns, not even by the sense of the coming sundering. Distrust—loneliness—the one was past, even if the other were to come!

The hotel-portier handed me a telegram, as we halted in the light of the doorway.

"Wait till I read this," I said.

The dispatch ran: "Situation changed. Your coming unnecessary. Await my letter. Am starting for Scotland."

I gave an exclamation of pleasure, and translated the words to Imre.

"What! Then you need not leave Szent-Istvánhely?" he asked quickly, in the tone of heartiest pleasure that a friend could wish to hear. "Teremtette! I am as happy as you!.... What a good thing, too, that we were so sensible as not to allow ourselves to make a dumpish, dismal afternoon of it, over there at the Z.... You see, I am right, my dear fellow.. I am always right!... Philosophy, divine philosophy! Nothing like it! It makes all the world go round."......

With which Imre touched his csákó, laughed his jolliest laugh, and hurried away to the Commando of the regiment.

I went upstairs, not aware of there being stairs to climb... unless they might be steps to the stars. In fact the stars, it seemed to me, could not only shine their clearest in Szent-Istvánhely; but, after all, could take clement as well as unfriendly courses, in mortal destiny.

III. FACES—HEARTS—SOULS.

"Think'st thou that I could bear to part
With thee?—and learn to halve my heart?"
"No more reproach, no more despair!"
      — BYRON

—

"Et deduxit eos in portum voluntatis sorum".
      — *Psalm. CVI, 30.*

Next morning, before I was dressed, came this note:

I have just received word that I must take my company out to the camp at once. Please excuse my not coming. It does not make so much difference, now that you are to stay. Will write you from the Camp. Only a few days absence. I shall think of you
Imre.
P. S. Please write me.

I was amused, as well as pleased, at this characteristic missive.

My day passed rather busily. I had not time to send even a card to Imre; I had no reason to do so. To my surprise, the omission was noticed. For, on the following morning I was in receipt of a lively military Ansichtskarte with a few words scratched on it; and at evening came the ensuing communication; which, by the by, was neither begun with the "address of courtesy", as the "Complete Letter-Book" calls it, nor ended with the "salute of ceremony", recommended by the same useful volume; they being both of them details which Imre had particularly told me he omitted with his intimate "friends who were not prigs." He wrote:

Well, how goes it with you? With me it is dull and fatiguing enough out here. You know how I hate all this business, even if you and Karvaly insist on my trying to like it. I have a great deal to say to you this evening that I really cannot write. Today was hot and it rained hard. Dear Oswald, you

72

do not know how I value your friendship. Yesterday I saw the very largest frog that ever was created. He looked the very image of our big vis-a-vis in the Casino, Hofkapellan Számbor. Why in God's name do you not write? The whole city is full of tiz-filléres picture-postcards! Buy one, charge it to my account, write me on it.——
Imre.
P. S. I think of you often, Oswald.

This communication, like its predecessor, was written in a tenth-century kind of hand, with a blunt lead-pencil! I sent its authour a few lines, of quite as laconical a tone as he had given me to understand he so much preferred.

The next day, yet another communication from the P... Camp! Three billets in as many days, from a person who "hated to write letters," and "never wrote them when he could get out of it!" Clearly, Imre in camp was not Imre in Szent-Istvánhely!

Thank you, dear Oswald, for your note. Do not think too much of that old nonsense (azon régi bolondság) about not writing letters. It depends. I send my this in a spare moment. But I have nothing whatever to say. Weather here warm and rainy. Oswald, you are a great deal in my thoughts. I hope I am often in yours. I shall not return tomorrow, but I intend to be with you on Sunday. Life is wearisome. But so long as one has a friend, one can get on with much that is part of the burden; or possibly with all of it.——Yours ever——
Imre

I have neglected to mention that the second person of intimate Magyar address, the "thou" and "thee", was used in these epistles of Imre, in my answers, with the same instinctiveness that had brought it to our lips on that evening in the Z... park. I shall not try to translate it systematically, however; any more than I shall note with system its disused English equivalents in the dialogue that occurs in the remainder of this record. More than once before the evening named, Imre and I had exchanged this familiarity, half in fun. But now it had come to stay. Thenceforth we adhered to it; a kind of serious symbolism as well as intimate sweetness in it.

I looked at that note with attention: first, because it was so opposed in tenor to the Imre von N... "model". Second, because there appeared to have been a stroke under the commonplace words "Yours ever". That stroke had been smirched out, or erased. Was it like Imre to be sentimental, for an instant, in a letter?—even in the most ordinary accent? Well, if he had given way to it, to try to conceal such a sign of the failing, particularly without re-writing the letter... why, that was characteristic enough! In sending him a newspaper-clipping, along with a word or so, I referred to the unnecessary briskness of our correspondence.

Pray do not trouble yourself, my dear N..., to change your habits on my account. Do not write, now or ever, only because a word from you is a pleasure to me. Besides I am not yet on my homeward-journey. Save your postal artillery.

To the foregoing from me, Imre's response was this:

It is three o'clock in the morning, and everybody in this camp must be sound asleep, except your most humble servant. You know that I sometimes do not sleep well, Lord knows why. So I sit here, and scrawl this to thee, dear Oswald... All the more willingly because I am awfully out of sorts with myself..... I have nothing special to write thee; and nevertheless how much I would now be glad to say to thee, were we together. See, dearest friend... thou hast walked from that other world of thine into my life, and I have taken my place in thine, because for thee and for me there shall be, I believe, a happiness henceforth that not otherwise could come to us. I have known what it is to suffer, just because there has been no man to whom I could speak or write as to thee. Dear friend, we are much to one another, and we shall be more and more... No, would not write if it were not a pleasure to me to do it. I promise thee so. We had a great regimental athletic contest this afternoon, and I took two prizes. I will try to sleep now, for I must be on my feet very early. Good night, or rather good-morning, and remember...
Thine own
Imre.

This letter gave me many reflections. There was no need for its closing injunction. To tell the truth, Imre von N... was beginning to bewilder me!—this Imre of the P... Camp and of the mail-bag, so unlike the Imre of our daily conversations and moods when vis-à-vis. There was certainly a curious, a growing psychic difference. The naïveté, the sincerity of the speaking and of the acting Imre was written into his lines spontaneously enough. But there was that odd new touch of an equally spontaneous something, a suppressed emotion—that I could not define. My own letters to Imre certainly did not ring to the like key. On the contrary (I may as well mention that it was not of mere accident, but in view of a resolution carefully considered, and held-to) the few lines which I sent him during those days were wholly lacking in any such personal utterances as his. If Imre chose to be inconsistent, I would be steadfast.

All such cogitations as to Imre's letters were however soon unnecessary, inasmuch as on the tenth day of his Camp-service, he wrote:

Expect me tomorrow. I am well. I have much to tell thee. After all, a camp is not a bad place for reflections. It is a tiresome, rainy day here. I took the second prize for shooting at long range today.
Imre

Now, I did not suppose that Imre's pent-up communicativeness was likely to burst out on the topic of the Hungarian local weather, much less with reference to his feats with a rifle, or in lifting heavy weights. I certainly could not fancy just what meditations promoted that remark about the Camp! So far as I knew anything, of such localities, camps were not favourable to much consecutive thinking except about the day's work.

I did not expect him till the afternoon should close. I was busy with my English letters. It was a warm August noon, and even when coat and waistcoat had been thrown aside, I was oppressed. My high-ceiled, spacious room was certainly amongst the cooler corners of Szent-Istvánhely; but the typical ardour of any Central-Hungary midsummer is almost Italian. Outside, in the hotel-court, the fountain trickled sleepily. Even the river steamers seemed too torpid to signal loudly. But suddenly there came a most wide-awake sort of knock; and Imre, with an exclamation of delight—Imre, erect, bronzed, flushed, with eyes flashing—with that smile of his which was almost as flashing as his eyes—Imre, more beautiful than ever, came to me, with both hands outstretched.

"At last.... and really!" I exclaimed as he hurried over the wide room, fairly beaming, as with contentment at being once more out of camp-routine. "And back five hours ahead of time!"

"Five hours ahead of time indeed!" he echoed, laughing. "Thou art glad? I know I am!"

"Dear Imre, I am immeasurably happy", I replied.

He leaned forward, and lightly kissed my cheek.

What!—he Imre von N—, who so had questioned the warm-hearted greetings of his friend—Captain M—! An odd lapse indeed!

"I am in a state of regular shipwreck," he exclaimed; standing up particularly straight again, after a demonstration that so confounded me as to leave me wordless!— "I have had no breakfast, no luncheon, nothing to eat since five o'clock. I am tired as a dog, and hungry—oh, mint egy vén Kárpáti medve!" [Literally, "as an old Carpathian bear".] "I stopped to have a bath at the Officers' Baths.. you should see the dust between here and the Camp... and to change, and write a note to my father. So, if you don't mind, the sooner I have something to eat and perhaps a nap, why the better. I am done up!"

In a few moments we were at table. Imre manifestly was not too fagged to talk and laugh a great deal; with a truly Homeric exhibition of his appetite. The budget of experiences at the Camp was immediately drawn upon, with much vivacity. But as luncheon ended, my guest admitted that the fatigues of the hot morning-march with his troop, from P.... (during which several sunstrokes had occurred, those too-ordinary incidents of Hungarian army-movements in summer) were reacting on him. So I went to the Bank, as usual, for letters; transacted some other business on the way; and left Imre to himself. When I returned to my room an hour or so later, he was stretched out, sound asleep, on the long green sofa. His sword and his close-fitting fatigue-blouse were thrown on a chair. The collarless, unstarched shirt (that is so much an improvement on our civilian garment) was unbuttoned at the throat; the sleeves rolled up to his shoulders, in unconscious emphasizing of the deepened sun-tan of his fine skin. The long brown eye-lashes lying motionless, against his cheek, his physical abandonment, his deep, regular, soundless breathing... all betokened how the day had spent itself on his young strength. Once left alone, he had fallen asleep where he had sat down.

A great and profoundly human poet, in one famous scene, speaks of those emotions that come to us when we are watching, in his sleep, a human being that we love. Such moments are indeed likely to be subduing to many a sensitive man and woman. They bring before our eyes the effect of a living statue; of a beauty self-unconscious, almost abstract, if the being that we love be beautiful. Strongly, suddenly, comes also the hint at helplessness; the suggestion of protection from us, however less robust. Or the idea of the momentary but actual absence of that other soul from out of the body before us, a vanishing of that spirit to whom we ourselves cling. We feel a subconscious sense of the inevitable separation forever, when there shall occur the Silence of "the Breaker of Bonds, the Sunderer of Companionships, the Destroyer of Fellowships, the Divider of Hearts"—as (like a knell of everything earthly and intimate!) the old Arabian phrases lament the merciless divorce of death!

I stood and watched Imre a moment, these things in my mind. Then, moving softly about the room, lest he should be aroused, I began changing my clothes for the afternoon. But more than once the spell of my sleeping guest drew me to his side. At last, scarce half dressed, I sat down before him, to continue to look at him. Yes.. his face had the same expression now, as he slumbered there, that I had often remarked in his most silent moments of waking. There were not only the calm regular beauty, the manly uprightness, his winning naïveté of character written all through such outward charm for me; but along with that came again the appealing hint of an inward sadness; the shadow of some enrooted, hidden sorrow that would not pass, however proudly concealed.

"God bless thee, Imre!" my heart exclaimed in benediction, "God bless thee, and make thee happy!... happier than I! Thou hast given me thy friendship. I shall never ask of God... of Fate... anything more... save that the gift endure till we two endure not!"

The wish was like an echo from the Z... park. Or, rather, it was an echo from a time far earlier in my life. Once again, with a mystic certainty, I realized that those days of Solitude were now no longer of any special tyranny upon my moods. That was at an end for me, verily! O, my God! That was at an end!....

Imre opened his eyes.

"Great Árpád!", he exclaimed, smiling sleepily, "is it so late? You are dressing for the evening!"

"It is five o'clock," I answered. "But what difference does that make? Don't budge. Go to sleep again, if you choose. You need not think of getting supper at home. We will go to the F— Restaurant."

"So be it. And perhaps I shall ask you to keep me till morning, my dear fellow! I am no longer sleepy, but somehow or other I do feel most frightfully knocked-out! Those country roads are misery..... And I am a poor sleeper often,.... that it is, in a way. I get to worrying... to wondering over all sorts of things that there's no good in studying about... in daylight or dark."

"You never told me till lately, in one of your letters, that you were so much of an insomniac, Imre. Is it new?"

"Not in the least new. I have not wished to say anything about it to anybody. What's the use! Oh, there many are things that I haven't had time to tell you—things I have not spoken about with anyone—just as is the case with most men of sense in this world... eh? But do you know," he went on, sitting up and continuing with a manner more and more reposeful, thoughtful, strikingly unlike his ordinary nervous self, ".. but do you know that I have come back from the Camp to you, my dear Oswald, certain that I shall never be so restless and troubled a creature again. Thanks to you. For you see, so much that I have shut into myself I know now that I can trust to your heart. But give me a little time. To have a friend to trust myself to wholly—that is new to me."

I was deeply touched. I felt certain again that a change of some sort—mysterious, profound—had come over Imre, during those few days at the Camp. Something had happened. I recognized the mood of his letters. But what had evolved or disclosed it?

"Yes, my dear von N..." I returned, "your letters have said that, in a way, to me. How shall I thank you for your confidence, as well as for your affection?"

"Ah, my letters! Bother my letters! They said nothing much! You know I cannot write letters at all. What is more, you have been believing that I wrote you as... as a sort of duty. That whatever I said—or a lot of it—well, there were things which you fancied were not really I. I understood why you could think it."

"I never said that, Imre," I replied, sitting down beside him on the sofa.

"Not in so many words. But my guilty conscience prompted me. I mean that word, 'conscience', Oswald. For—I have not been fair to you, not honest. The only excuse is that I have not been honest with myself. You have thought me cold, reserved, abrupt... a fantastic sort of friend to you. One who valued you, and yet could hardly speak out his esteem—a careless fellow into whose life you have taken only surface-root. That isn't all. You have believed that I... that I... never could comprehend things... feelings... which you have lived through to the full... have suffered from... with every beat of your heart. But you are mistaken."

"I have no complaint against you, dear Imre." No, no! God knows that!

"No? But I have much against myself. That evening in the Z... park... you remember... when you were telling me"...

I interrupted him sharply: "Imre!"

He continued— "That evening in the Z— park when you were telling me"—

"Imre, Imre! You forget our promise!"

"No, I do not forget! It was a one-sided bargain, I am free to break it for a moment, nem igaz? Well then, I break it! There!

79

Dear friend, if you have ever doubted that I have a heart,... that I would trust you utterly, that I would have you know me as I am.... then from this afternoon forget to doubt! I have hid myself from you, because I have been too proud to confess myself not enough for myself! I have sworn a thousand times that I could and would bear anything alone—alone—yes, till I should die. Oswald—for God's sake—for our friendship's sake—do not care less for me because I am weary of struggling on thus alone! I shall not try to play hero, even to myself... not any longer. Oswald..., listen... you told me your story. Well, I have a story to tell you... Then you will understand. Wait... wait... one moment!... I must think how, where, to begin. My story is short compared with yours, and not so bitter; yet it is no pleasant one."

As he uttered the last few words, seated there beside me, whatever sympathy I could ever feel for any human creature went out to him, unspeakably. For, now, now, the trouble flashed into my mind! Of course it was to be the old, sad tale—he loved, loved unhappily—a woman!

The singer! The singer of Prag! That wife of his friend Karvaly. The woman whose fair and magnetic personality, had wrought unwittingly or wittingly, her inevitable spell upon him! One of those potent and hopeless passions, in which love, and probably loyalty to Karvaly, burdened this upright spirit with an irremediable misfortune!

"Well," I said very gently, "tell me all that you can, if there be one touch of comfort and relief for you in speaking, Imre. I am wholly yours, you know, for every word."

Instead of answering me at once, as he sat there so close beside me, supporting his bowed head on one hand, and with his free arm across my shoulder, he let the arm fall more heavily about me. Turning his troubled eyes once—so appealingly, so briefly!—on mine, he laid his face upon my breast. And then, I heard him murmur, as if not to me only, but also to himself:

"O, thou dear friend! Who bringest me, as none have brought it before thee... rest!"

Rest? Not rest for me! A few seconds of that pathetic, trusting nearness which another man could have sustained so calmly... a few instants of that unspeakable joy in realizing how much more I was in his life than I had dared to conceive possible... just those few throbs upon my heart of that weary spirit of my friend... and then the Sex-Demon brought his storm upon my traitorous nature, in fire and lava! I struggled in shame and despair to keep down the hateful physical passion which was making nothing of all my psychic loyalty, asserting itself against my angriest will. In vain! The defeat must come; and, worse, it must be understood by Imre. I started up. I thrust Imre from me—falling away from him, escaping from his side—knowing that just in his surprise at my abruptness, I must meet—his detection of my miserable weakness. No words can express my self-disgust. Once on my feet, I staggered to the opposite side of the round table between us. I dropped into a chair. I could not raise my eyes to Imre. I could not speak. Everything was vanishing about me. Of only one thing could I be certain; that now all was over between us! Oh, this cursed outbreak and revelation of my sensual weakness! this inevitable physical appeal of Imre to me! This damned and inextricable ingredient in the chemistry of what ought to be wholly a spiritual drawing toward him, but which meant that I— desired my friend for his gracious, virile beauty—as well as loved him for his fair soul! Oh, the shame of it all, the uselessness of my newest resolve to be more as the normal man, not utterly the Uranian! Oh, the folly of my oaths to love Imre without that thrill of the plain sexual Desire, that would be a sickening horror to him! All was over! He knew me for what I was. He would have none of me. The flight of my dreams, departing in a torn cloud together, would come with the first sound of his voice!

But Imre did not speak. I looked up. He had not stirred. His hand was still lying on the table, with its open palm to me! And oh, there was that in his face... in the look so calmly bent upon me... that was... good God above us!.. so kind!

"Forgive me," I said. "Forgive me! Perhaps you can do that. Only that. You see... you know now. I have tried to change myself... to care for you only with my soul. But I cannot change. I will go from you. I will go to the other end of the world. Only do not believe that what I feel for you is wholly base... that were you not outwardly—what you are—had I less of my terrible sensitiveness to your mere beauty, Imre—I would care less for your friendship. God knows that I love you and respect you as a man loves and respects his friend. Yes, yes, a thousand times! But... but... nevertheless... Oh, what shall I say... You could never understand! So no use! Only I beg you not to despise me too deeply for my weakness; and when you remember me, pardon me for the sake of the friendship bound up in the love, even if you shudder at the love which curses the friendship."

Imre smiled. There was both bitterness as well as sweetness in his face now. But the bitterness was not for me. His voice broke the short silence in so intense a sympathy, in a note of such perfect accord, such unchanged regard, that I could scarcely master my eyes in hearing him. He clasped my hand.

"Dear Oswald! Brother indeed of my soul and body! Why dost thou ask me to forgive thee! Why should I 'forgive'? For—oh, Oswald, Oswald! I am just as art thou... I am just as art thou!"

"Thou! Just as I am? I do not understand!"

"But that will be very soon, Oswald. I tell thee again that I am as thou art... wholly.. wholly! Canst thou really not grasp the truth, dear friend? Oh, I wish with all my heart that I had not so long held back my secret from thee! It is I who must ask forgiveness. But at least I can tell thee today that I came back to thee to give thee confidence for confidence, heart for heart, Oswald! before this day should end. With no loss of respect— no weakening of our friendship. No, no! Instead of that, only with more—with... with all!"

"Imre... Imre! I do not understand—I do not dare... to understand."

"Look into thyself, Oswald! It is all there. I am an Uranian, as thou art. From my birth I have been one. Wholly, wholly homosexual, Oswald! The same fire, the same, that smoulders or flashes in thee! It was put into my soul and body too, along with whatever else is in them that could make me wish to win the sympathy of just such a friend as thee, or make thee wish to seek mine. My youth was like thine; and to become older, to grow up to be a man in years, a man in every sinew and limb of my body, there was no changing of my nature in that. There were only the bewilderments, concealments, tortures that come to us. There is nothing, nothing, that any man can teach me of what is one's life with it all. How well I know it! That inborn mysterious, frightful sensitiveness to whatever is the man—that eternal vague yearning and seeking for the unity that can never come save by a love that is held to be a crime and a shame! The instinct that makes us cold toward the woman, even to hating her, when one thinks of her as a sex. And the mask, the eternal mask! to be worn before our fellowmen for fear that they should spit in our faces in their loathing of us! Oh God, I have known it all—I have understood it all!"

It was indeed my turn to be silent now. I found myself yet looking at him in incredulity—wordless.

"But that is not the whole of my likeness to thee, Oswald. For, I have endured that cruellest of torments for us—which fell also to thy lot. I believe it to be over now, or soon wholly so to be. But the remembrance of it will not soon pass, even with thy affection to heal my heart. For I too have loved a man, loved him—hiding my passion from him under the coldness of a common friendship. I too have lived side by side, day by day, with him; in terror, lest he should see what he was to me, and so drive me from him. Ah, I have been unhappier, too, than thou, Oswald. For I must needs to watch his heart, as something not merely impossible for me to possess (I would have cast away my soul to possess it!)—but given over to a woman—laid at her feet—with daily less and less of thought for what was his life with me... Oh, Oswald!... the wretchedness of it is over now, God be thanked! and not a little so because I have found thee, and thou hast found me. But only to think of it again"....

He paused as if the memory were indeed wormwood. I understood now! And oh, what mattered it that I could not yet understand or excuse the part that he had played before me for so long?—his secrecy almost inexplicable if he had had so much as a guess at my story, my feelings for him! As in a dream, believing, disbelieving, fearing, rejoicing, trembling, rapt, I began to understand Fate!

Yet, mastering my own exultant heart, I wished in those moments to think only of him. I asked gently:

"You mean your friend Karvaly?"

"Even so... Karvaly."

"O, my poor, poor Imre! My brother indeed! Tell me all. Begin at the beginning."

I shall not detail all of Imre's tale. There was little in it for the matter of that, which could be set forth here as outwardly dramatic. Whoever has been able, by nature or accident, to know, in a fairly intimate degree, the workings of the similisexual and uranistic heart; whoever has marvelled at them, either in sympathy or antipathy, even if merely turning over the pages of psychiatric treatises dealing with them—he would find nothing specially unfamiliar in such biography. I will mention here, as one of the least of the sudden discoveries of that afternoon, the fact that Imre had some knowledge of such literature, whether to his comfort or greater melancholy, according to his author. Also he had formally consulted one eminent Viennese specialist who certainly was much wiser—far less positive—and not less calming than my American theorist.

The great Viennese psychiater had not recommended marriage to Imre: recognizing in Imre's "case" that inborn homosexualism that will not be dissipated by wedlock; but perhaps only intensifies, and so is surer to darken irretrievably the nuptial future of husband and wife, and to visit itself on their children after them. But the Austrian doctor had not a little comforted and strengthened Imre morally; warning him away from despising himself: from thinking himself alone, and a sexual Pariah; from over-morbid sufferings; from that bitterness and despair which, year by year, all over the world, can explain, in hundreds of cases, the depressed lives, the lonely existences, the careers mysteriously interrupted—broken? What Asmodeus could look into the real causes (so impenetrably veiled) of sudden and long social exiles; of sundered ties of friendship or family; of divorces that do not disclose their true ground? Longer still would be the chronicle of ruined peace of mind, tranquil lives maddened, fortunes shattered—by some merciless blackmailer who trades on his victim's secret! Darker yet the "mysterious disappearances," the sudden suicides "wholly inexplicable," the strange, fierce crimes—that are part of the daily history of hidden uranianism, of the battle between the homosexual man and social canons—or of the battle with just himself! Ah, these dramas of the Venus Urania! played out into death, in silent but terribly-troubled natures!—among all sorts and conditions of men!

C'est Venus, tout entière à sa proie attachée

Imre's youth had been, indeed, one long and lamentable obsession of precocious, inborn homosexuality. Imre (just as in many instances) had never been a weakling, an effeminate lad, nor cared for the society of the girls about him on the playground or in the house. On the contrary, his sexual and social indifference or aversion to them had been always thoroughly consistent with the virile emotions of that sort. But there had been the boy-friendships that were passions; the sense of his being out of key with his little world in them; the deepening certitude that there was a mystery in himself that "nobody would understand"; some element rooted in him that was mocked by the whole boy-world, by the whole man-world. A part of himself to be crushed out, if it could be crushed, because base and vile. Or that, at any rate, was to be forever hid.. hid.. hid.. for his life's sake hid! So Imre had early put on the Mask; the Mask that millions never lay by till death—and many not even then!

And in Imre's case there had come no self-justification till late in his sorrowful young manhood. Not until quite newly, when he had discovered how the uranistic nature is regarded by men who are wiser and wider-minded than our forefathers were, had Imre accepted himself as an excusable bit of creation.

Fortunately, Imre had not been born and brought up in an Anglo-Saxon civilization; where is still met, at every side, so dense a blending of popular ignorances; of century-old and century-blind religious and ethical misconceptions, of unscientific professional conservatism in psychiatric circles, and of juristic barbarisms; all, of course, accompanied with the full measure of British or Yankee social hypocrisy toward the daily actualities of homosexualism. By comparison, indeed, any other lands and races—even those yet hesitant in their social toleration or legal protection of the Uranian—seem educative and kindly; not to distinguish peoples whose attitude is distinctively one of national common-sense and humanity. But in this sort of knowledge, as in many another, the world is feeling its way forward (should one say back?) to intelligence, to justice and to sympathy, so spirally, so unwillingly! It is not yet in the common air.

Twice Imre had been on the point of suicide. And though there had been experiences in the Military-Academy, and certain much later ones to teach him that he was not unique in Austria-Hungary, in Europe, or the world, still unluckily, Imre had got from them (as is too often the hap of the Uranian) chiefly the sense of how widely despised, mocked, and loathed is the Uranian Race. Also how sordid and debasing are the average associations of the homosexual kind, how likely to be wanting in idealism, in the exclusiveness, in those pure and manly influences which ought to be bound up in them and to radiate from them! He had grown to have a horror of similisexual types, of all contacts with them. And yet, until lately, they could not be torn entirely out of his life. Most Uranists know why!

Still, they had been so expelled, finally. The turning-point had come with Karvaly. It meant the story of the development of a swift, admiring friendship from the younger soldier toward the older. But alas! this had gradually become a fierce, despairing homosexual love. This, at its height, had been as destructive of Imre's peace as it was hopeless. Of course, it was impossible of confession to its object. Karvaly was no narrow intellect; his affection for Imre was warm. But he would never have understood, not even as some sort of a diseased illusion, this sentiment in Imre. Much less would he have tolerated it for an instant. The inevitable rupture of their whole intimacy would have come with Imre's betrayal of his passion. So he had done wisely to hide every throb from Karvaly. How sharply Karvaly had on one occasion expressed himself on masculine homosexuality, Imre cited to me, with other remembrances. At the time of the vague scandal about the ex-officer Clement, whom Imre and I had met, Imre had asked Karvaly, with a fine carelessness,— "Whether he believed that there was any scientific excuse for such a sentiment?" Karvaly answered, with the true conviction of the dionistic temperament that has never so much as paused to think of the matter as a question in psychology... "If I found that you cared for another man that way, youngster, I should give you my best revolver, and tell you to put a bullet through your brains within an hour! Why, if I found that you thought of me so, I should brand you in the Officers Casino tonight, and shoot you myself at ten paces tomorrow morning. Men are not to live when they turn beasts.... Oh, damn your doctors and scientists! A man's a man, and a woman's a woman! You can't mix up their emotions like that."

The dread of Karvaly's detection, the struggle with himself to subdue passion, not merely to hide it, and along with these nerve-wearing solicitudes, the sense of what the suspicion of the rest of the world about him would inevitably bring on his head, had put Imre, little by little, into a sort of panic. He maintained an exaggerated attitude of safety, that had wrought on him unluckily, in many a valuable social relation. He wore his mask each and every instant; resolving to make it his natural face before himself! Having, discovered, through intimacy with Karvaly how a warm friendship on the part of the homosexual temperament, over and over takes to itself the complexion of homosexual love—the one emotion constantly likely to rise in the other and to blend itself inextricably into its alchemy—Imre had simply sworn to make no intimate friendship again! This, without showing himself in the least unfriendly; indeed with his being more hail-fellow-well-met with his comrades than otherwise.

But there Imre stopped! He bound his warm heart in a chain, he vowed indifference to the whole world, he assisted no advances of warm, particular regard from any comrade. He became that friend of everybody in general who is the friend of nobody in particular! He lived in a state of perpetual defence in his regiment, and in whatever else was social to him in Szent-Istvánhely. So surely as he admired another man—would gladly have won his generous and virile affection—Imre turned away from that man! He covered this morbid state of self-inclusion, this solitary life (such it was, apart from the relatively short intimacy with Karvaly) with laughter and a most artistic semblance of brusqueness; of manly preoccupation with private affairs. Above all, with the skilful cultivation of his repute as a Lothario who was nothing if not sentimental and absorbed in— woman! This is possibly the most common device, as it is the securest, on the part of an Uranian. Circumstances favoured Imre in it; and he gave it its full show of honourable mystery. The cruel irony of it was often almost humorous to Imre.

"... They have given me the credit of being the most confirmed rake in high life... think of that! I, and in high life!.. to be found in town. The less they could trace as ground for it, why, so much the stronger rumours!.. you know how that sort of a label sticks fast to one, once pinned on. Especially if a man is really a gentleman and holds his tongue, ever and always, about his intimacies with women. Why, Oswald, I have never felt that I could endure to be alone five minutes with any woman... I mean in—that way! Not even with a woman most dear to me, as many, many women are. Not even with a wife that loved me. I have never had any intimacies—not one—of that sort... Merely semblances of such! Queer experiences I've tumbled into with them, too! You know."

Oh, yes... I knew!

Part of Imre's exaggerated, artificial bearing toward the outer world was the nervous shrinking from commonplace social demonstrativeness on the part of his friends. To that mannerism I have already referred. It had become a really important accent, I do not doubt, in Imre's acting-out of a friendly, cheerful, yet keep-your-distance sort of personality. But there was more than that in it.

It was a detail in the effort toward his self-transformation; a minor article in his compact with himself never to give up the struggle to "cure" himself. He was convinced that this was the most impossible of achievements. But he kept on fighting for it. And since one degree of sentiment led so treacherously to another, why, away with all!

"But Imre, I do not yet see why you have not trusted me sooner. There have been at least two moments in our friendship when you could have done so; and one of them was when.. you should!"

"Yes, you are right. I have been unkind. But then, I have been as unkind to myself. The two times you speak of, Oswald... you mean, for one of them, that night that we met Clement... and spoke about such matters for a moment while we were crossing the Lánczhid? And the other chance was after you had told me your own story, over there in the Z... park?"

"Yes. Of course, the fault is partly mine—once. I mean that time on the Bridge... I fenced you off from me—I misled you—didn't help you—I didn't help myself. But even so, you kept me at sword's length, Imre! You wore your mask so closely—gave me no inch of ground to come nearer to you, to understand you, to expect anything except scorn—our parting! Oh, Imre! I have been blind, yes! but you have been dumb."

"You wonder and you blame me," he replied, after busying himself a few seconds with his own perplexing thoughts. "Again, I say 'Forgive me.' But you must remember that we played at cross-purposes too much (as I now look back on what we said that first time) for me to trust myself to you. I misunderstood you. I was stupid—nervous. It seemed to me certain, at first, that you had me in your mind—that I was the friend you spoke of—laughed at, in a way. But after I saw that I was mistaken? Oh, well it appeared to me that, after all, you must be one of the Despisers. Gentler-hearted than the most; broader minded, in a way; but one who, quite likely, thought and felt as the rest of the world. I was afraid to go a word farther! I was afraid to lose you. I shivered afterward, when I remembered that I had spoken then of what I did. Especially about that man... who cared for me once upon a time... in that way... And so suddenly to meet Clement! I didn't know he was in Szent-Istvánhely; the meeting took me by surprise. I heard next morning that his mother had been very ill."

"But afterwards, Imre? You surely had no fear of what you call 'losing' me then? How could you possibly meet my story—in that hour of such bitter confidence from me!—as you did? Could come no further toward me? When you were certain that to find you my Brother in the Solitude would make you the nearer-beloved and dearer-prized!"

"That's harder for me to answer. For one reason, it was part of that long battle with myself! It was something against the policy of my whole life!... as I had sworn to live it for all the rest of it... before myself or the world. I had broken that pledge already in our friendship, such as even then it was! Broken it suddenly, completely... before realizing what I did. The feeling that I was weak, that I cared for you, that I was glad that you sought my friendship... ah, the very sense of nearness and companionship in that... But I fought with all that, I tell you! Pride, Oswald!... a fool's pride! My determination to go on alone, alone, to make myself sufficient for myself, to make my punishment my tyrant!—to be martyred under it! Can you not understand something of that? You broke down my pride that night, dear Oswald. Oh, then I knew that I had found the one friend in the world, out of a million-million men not for me! And nevertheless I hung back! The thought of your going from me had been like a knife-stroke in my heart all the evening long. But yet I could not speak out. All the while I understood how our parting was a pain to you—I could have echoed every thought that was in your soul about it!... but I would not let myself speak one syllable to you that could show you that I cared! No!... then I would have let you go away in ignorance of everything that was most myself... rather than have opened that life-secret, or my heart, as we sat there. Oh, it was as if I was under a spell, a cursed enchantment that would mean a new unhappiness, a deeper silence for the rest of my life! But the wretched charm was perfect. Good God!... what a night I passed! The mood and the moment had been so fit... yet both thrown away! My heart so shaken, my tongue so paralyzed! But before morning came,

Oswald, that fool's hesitation was over. I was clear and resolved, the devil of arrogance had left me. I was amazed at myself. You would have heard everything from me that day. But the call to the Camp came. I had not a moment. I could not write what I wished. There was nothing to do but to wait."

"The waiting has done no harm, Imre."

"And there is another reason, Oswald, why I found it hard to be frank with you. At least, I think so. It is—what shall call it?—the psychic trace of the woman in me. Yes, after all, the woman! The counter-impulse, the struggle of the weakness that is womanishness itself, when one has to face any sharp decision... to throw one's whole being into the scale! Oh, I know it, I have found it in me before now! I am not as you, the Uranian who is too much man! I am more feminine in impulse—of weaker stuff... I feel it with shame. You know how the woman says 'no' when she means 'yes' with all her soul! How she draws back from the arms of the man that she loves when she dreams every night of throwing herself into them? How she finds herself doing, over and over, just that which is against her thought, her will, her duty! I tell you, there is something of that in me, Oswald! I must make it less... you must help me. It must be one of the good works of your friendship, of your love, for me. Oh, Oswald, Oswald!... you are not only to console me for all that I have suffered, for anything in my past that has gone wrong. For, you are to help me to make myself over, indeed, in all that is possible, whatever cannot be so."

"We must help each other Imre. But do not speak so of woman, my brother! Sexually, we may not value her. We may not need her, as do those Others. But think of the joy that they find in her to which we are cold; the ideals from which we are shut out! Think of your mother, Imre; as I think of mine! Think of the queens and peasants who have been the light and the glory of races and peoples. Think of the gentle, noble sisters and wives, the serene, patient rulers of myriad homes. Think of the watching nurses in the hospitals... of the spirits of mercy who walk the streets of plague and foulness!... think of the nun on her knees for the world...!"

The shadows in the room were almost at their deepest. We were still sitting face to face, almost without having stirred since that moment when I had quitted his side so suddenly—to divine how much closer I was to be drawn to him henceforth. Life!—Life and Death!—Life—Love—Death! The sense of eternal kinship in their mystery.... somehow it haunted one then! as it is likely to do when not our unhappiness but a kind of over-joy swiftly oppresses us; making us to feel that in some other sphere, and if less grossly "set within this muddy vesture of decay," we might understand all three... might find all three to be one! Life—Love—Death!...

"Oswald, you will never go away from me!"

"Imre, I will never go away from thee. Thy people shall be mine. Thy King shall be mine. Thy country shall be mine,—thy city mine! My feet are fixed! We belong together. We have found what we had despaired of finding... 'the friendship which is love, the love which is friendship'. Those who cannot give it—accept it—let them live without it. It can be 'well, and very well' with them. Go they their ways without it! But for Us, who for our happiness or unhappiness cannot think life worth living if lacking it... for Us, through the world's ages born to seek it in pain or joy... it is the highest, holiest Good in the world. And for one of us to turn his back upon it, were to find he would better never have been born!"

It was eleven o'clock. Imre and I had supped and taken a stroll in the yellow moonlight, along the quais, overlooking the shimmering Duna; and on through the little Erzsébet-tér where we had met, a few weeks ago—it seemed so long ago! I had heard more of Imre's life and individuality as a boy; full of the fine and unhappy emotions of the uranistic youth. We had laughed over his stock of experiences in the Camp. We had talked of things grave and gay.

Then we had sauntered back. It was chance; but lo! we were on the Lánczhid, once more! The Duna rippled and swirled below. The black barges slumbered against the stone rakpartok. The glittering belts of the city-lights flashed in long perspectives along the wide river's sweeping course and twinkled from square to square, from terrace to terrace. Across from us, at a garden-café, a cigány orchestra was pulsating; crying out, weeping, asking, refusing, wooing, mocking, inebriating, despairing, triumphant! All the warm Magyar night about us was dominated by those melting chromatics, poignant cadences—those harmonies eternally oriental, minor-keyed, insidious, nerve-thrilling. The arabesques of the violins, the vehement rhythms of the clangorous czimbalom!.... Ah, this time on the Lánczhid, neither for Imre nor me was it the sombre Bakony song, "O jaj! az álom nelkül"—but instead the free, impassioned leap and acclaim,— "Huszár legény vagyok!—Huszár legény vagyok!"

We were back in the quiet room, lighted now only by the moon. Far up, on the distant Pálota heights, the clear bell of Szent-Mátyás struck the three-quarters. The slow notes filled the still night like a benediction, keyed to that haunting, divine, prophetic triad, Life—Love—Death! Benediction threefold and supreme to the world!

"Oh, my brother! Oh, my friend!" exclaimed Imre softly, putting his arm about me and holding me to his heart. "Listen to me. Perhaps.. perhaps even yet, canst thou err in one, only one thought. I would have thee sure that when I am with thee here, now, I miss nothing and no one—I seek nothing and no one! My quest, like thine, is over!... I wish no one save thee, dear Oswald, no one else, even as I feel thou wishest none save me, henceforth. I would have thee believe that I am glad just as thou art glad. Alike have we two been sad because of our lonely hearts, our long restlessness of soul and body, our vain dreams, our worship of this or that hope—vision—which has been kept far from us—it may be, overvalued by us! We have suffered so much thou and I!... because of what never could be! We shall be all the happier now for what is real for us... I love thee, as thou lovest me. I have found, as thou hast found, 'the friendship which is love, the love which is friendship.'... Come then, O friend! O brother, to our rest! Thy heart on mine, thy soul with mine! For us two it surely is... Rest!"

Truth? What is truth? Two human hearts
Wounded by men, by fortune tried.
Outwearied with their lonely parts.
Vow to beat henceforth side by side.
— Matthew Arnold

THE END

About the author:

Edward Irenaeus Prime-Stevenson. Originally published in 1906 and written while Prime-Stevenson was living as an expatriate in Europe, the novel is a ground-breaking, positive story of romance between two men.

Throughout his career, Prime-Stevenson sought to dispel falsehoods surrounding the history of homosexuality. Writing under the pseudonym Xavier Mayne, Prime-Stevenson took great care to insulate himself from the reprisal common to the period in which he worked.

Despite the initial printing being limited to only 500 copies Prime-Stevenson is now recognized as a pioneering advocate for the rights of the LGBTQI community.

More books from Fahrenheit Press

The Beloved Children

Three young women; Chrysanthemum, Rose & Orage are thrown together performing as The Three Graces on the stage of Fankes' Theatre during the closing days of the Second World War.

It's there they come under the spell of wardrobe mistresses Dolores and Janna – a chance encounter that will guide and change all of their fates forever.

Set in the dying days of vaudeville theatre and laced with mysticism, fortune tellers, ghosts, and evocative descriptions of the closing days of the War - The Beloved Children will literally make you laugh out loud and perhaps even shed the odd tear.

The Beloved Children is wise, funny, heart-breaking, joyous, poignant, and entirely entirely enthralling.

Tina Jackson has conjured characters that you will fall unapologetically in love with and placed them in a world that you won't want to leave.

This book genuinely weaves a spell around the reader and once you make friends with Janna, Dolores, and The Three Graces you'll never want to be without them in your life again.

"This gloriously offbeat tale has shades of Angela Carter, with its beguiling characters weaving a magical spell." - Kitty Marlow, The Mail On Sunday

Pure by Jo Perry

Caught in a pincer movement between the sudden death of Evelyn (her favourite aunt) and the Corona virus, Ascher Lieb finds herself unexpectedly locked down in her aunt's retirement community with only Evelyn's grief-stricken dog Freddie for company.

As the world tumbles down into a pandemic shaped rabbit-hole Ascher is wracked with guilt that her aunt was buried without the Jewish burial rights of purification.

In order to atone for this dereliction of familial duty, Ascher – in her own words 'a profane, unobservant, atheist Jew, frequent liar and grieving loser' –volunteers to become the newest member of Valley Haverim Chevra Kadisha, a Jewish burial society on-call twenty-four-seven during lockdown and performing Mitzvot at no cost to the bereaved.

What follows is a journey through the insanity of lockdown in Los Angeles as Ascher attempts to bring peace to a troubled soul, and perhaps in the end redemption for herself.

This novel is everything.

In the hands of a lesser-writer a novel set in the time of covid could lead to a cliché ridden trope-fest, but instead with the skill and grace we've come to expect from Jo Perry she has delivered a book that is wise and beautiful and uplifting.

In our opinion with *Pure*, Jo Perry has surpassed even her own high-bar and written the finest novel of her career to date – but don't take our word for it – here's what some of her fellow writers say…

"Faultlessly imagined and beautifully written, this is one of the best novels I've read all year." –Timothy Hallinan, author of the acclaimed Simeon Grist series

Black Moss by David Nolan

In April 1990, as rioters took over Strangeways prison in Manchester, someone killed a little boy at Black Moss.

And no one cared.

No one except Danny Johnston, an inexperienced radio reporter trying to make a name for himself.

More than a quarter of a century later, Danny returns to his home city to revisit the murder that's always haunted him.

If Danny can find out what really happened to the boy, maybe he can cure the emptiness he's felt inside since he too was a child.

But finding out the truth might just be the worst idea Danny Johnston has ever had.

"As one would expect from a writer with the skill and experience of David Nolan, this haunting book deals with very difficult issues in an incredibly sympathetic manner while at the same time throwing a light onto one of the most complicated and shaming areas of our society - the failure to protect those who are the most vulnerable."

The Perception of Dolls by Anthony Croix

"It's almost as if history is trying to erase the whole affair." - Anthony Croix

The triple murder and failed suicide that took place at 37 Fantoccini Street in 2001, raised little media interest at the time. In a week heavy with global news, a 'domestic tragedy' warranted few column inches. The case was open and shut, the inquest was brief and the 'Doll Murders' - little more than a footnote in the ledgers of Britain's true crime enthusiasts - were largely forgotten.

Nevertheless, investigations were made, police files generated, testimonies recorded, and conclusions reached. The reports are there, a matter of public record, for those with a mind to look.

The details of what took place in Fantoccini Street in the years that followed are less accessible. The people involved in the field trips to number 37 are often unwilling, or unable, to talk about what they witnessed. The hours of audio recordings, video tapes, written accounts, photographs, drawings, and even online postings are elusive, almost furtive.

In fact, were it not for a chance encounter between the late Anthony Croix and an obsessive collector of Gothic dolls, the Fantoccini Street Reports might well have been lost forever.

Cash Rules Everything Around Me by Rob Gittins

Morrissey Jarrett is fresh out of prison and back on the streets of his hometown Cardiff.

During his enforced absence the city has been re-developed to within an inch of its life and a disoriented Morrissey falls back into old habits as he scams, schemes, and steals whatever he needs to survive.

Morrissey has big dreams though. Dreams of making one last huge score, dreams of leaving his life of crime behind, dreams of reuniting with the love of his life and dreams of walking off into the sunset with her. Happy. Ever. After.

All he needs is a plan.

Luckily, the circles Morrissey frequents provide ample opportunities for ill-gotten gains and soon the perfect job literally falls into his hands.

And so, along with a hastily assembled crew of misfits, Morrissey embarks on planning the perfect heist. With all their eyes fixed steadily on a payday that could change their stars forever - all they have to do is keep their heads down, play it cool, and follow the plan to the letter.

What could possibly go wrong?

"Utterly compelling... highly recommended for those looking for a crime novel that is that bit different." -Newbooks magazine

"Visceral, strongly visual and beautifully structured... powerful, quirky characters." - Andrew Taylor, Winner, Crime Writers Association Cartier Diamond Dagger

"Impressive, hard-hitting, well-plotted and superbly written" - Crime Review

To read more of the best, most inspiring fiction in the world visit us at our website.

www.Fahrenheit-Press.com

9 781914 475559